Suddenly he met Mr. Panther. FRONTISPIECE. *See page 22.*

DOVER
CHILDREN'S THRIFT CLASSICS

Mother West Wind's Animal Friends

THORNTON W. BURGESS

Original Illustrations by George Kerr
Adapted by Pat Stewart

PUBLISHED IN ASSOCIATION WITH THE
THORNTON W. BURGESS MUSEUM AND THE
GREEN BRIAR NATURE CENTER, SANDWICH, MASSACHUSETTS,
BY
DOVER PUBLICATIONS, INC., MINEOLA, NEW YORK

DOVER CHILDREN'S THRIFT CLASSICS
EDITOR OF THIS VOLUME: JANET BAINE KOPITO

Bibliographical Note

This Dover edition, first published in 2003 in association with the Thornton W. Burgess Museum and the Green Briar Nature Center, Sandwich, Massachusetts, who have provided a new introduction, is an unabridged republication of the work originally published by Little, Brown, and Company, Boston, in 1912. The original George Kerr illustrations have been adapted for this new edition by Pat Stewart.

Library of Congress Cataloging-in-Publication Data

Burgess, Thornton W. (Thornton Waldo), 1874–1965.
  Mother West Wind's animal friends / Thornton W. Burgess ; original illustrations by George Kerr ; adapted by Pat Stewart.
    p. cm. — (Dover children's thrift classics)
  Reprint. Originally published: Boston : Little, Brown, 1912.
  Summary: Fifteen tales that explain how Prickly Porky got his quills, why Johnny Chuck ran away, the reason for Jerry Muskrat's new house, and other mysteries about the residents of the Green Meadow.
  ISBN 0-486-43030-8 (pbk.)
    1. Children's stories, American. [1. Animals—Fiction. 2. Short stories.] I. Kerr, George, ill. II. Stewart, Pat Ronson, ill. III. Title. IV. Series.

PZ7.B917L1 2003
[Fic]—dc21

                                                                2003046187

Manufactured in the United States of America
Dover Publications, Inc., 31 East 2nd Street, Mineola, N.Y. 11501

Introduction to the Dover Edition

There is a stranger in the Green Forest. He has short legs; he eats bark; and he has sharp quills sticking out of his fur. This creature can even roll up in a ball when threatened. Everyone in the Green Forest is curious about this new stranger! This is the tale of Prickly Porky the Porcupine. As you read this book, you will learn how he came to the Green Forest and won the respect of all the little meadow folk and forest animals. Prickly Porky is just one of the new characters that you will meet when reading *Mother West Wind's Animal Friends*. This book was written back in 1912 by children's author Thornton W. Burgess. Beginning in 1910, Mr. Burgess wrote over 170 different children's books.

Back in 1903, before Thornton Burgess wrote any of his books for children, a woman in East Sandwich, Massachusetts, started a business making jams and jellies. It was known as the Green Briar Jam Kitchen. For over 100 years, Jam Kitchen staff have made fine jams, jellies, pickles and marmalades using old-fashioned recipes. Today, the kitchen is the home of the Thornton W. Burgess Society's Green Briar Nature Center. The Thornton W. Burgess Society, a nonprofit environmental

education organization, purchased the property in 1979. Green Briar is located on the shore of the Smiling Pool and at the edge of the Briar Patch, locations familiar to readers of Thornton Burgess stories.

In fact, when Mr. Burgess started writing his popular children's books, he began telling people about his boyhood and what it was like to grow up in Sandwich. The staff of the Green Briar Jam Kitchen was besieged by children wanting to know where they could find Peter Rabbit and his Briar Patch. On a visit to Sandwich in 1939, Thornton Burgess stopped into Green Briar to pick up some jam and visit with the owner, Ida Putnam. He inscribed the following to Ida in one of his books: "To Ida, who is bothered by the Old Briar Patch inquiries. Too bad. But Peter lives there, and there is nothing I can do about it. It is a wonderful thing to sweeten the world that is in a jam and needs preserving." The Society continues to operate the Green Briar Jam Kitchen as a way to sweeten the world and help support the Society's programs. You can learn more about the Thornton Burgess Society and its facilities at its website: **www.thorntonburgess.org**.

Contents

List of Illustrations

IN TENDER, LOVING, REVERENT MEMORY OF MY MOTHER,
WHO LOVED LITTLE CHILDREN AND WAS BELOVED
OF THEM, AND TO WHOM I OWE A DEBT
OF AFFECTION AND OF GRATITUDE
BEYOND MY POWER TO PAY

I
The Merry Little Breezes Save
the Green Meadows

OLD Mother West Wind's family is very big, very big indeed. There are dozens and dozens of Merry Little Breezes, all children of Old Mother West Wind. Every morning she comes down from the Purple Hills and tumbles them out of a great bag on to the Green Meadows. Every night she gathers them into the great bag and, putting it over her shoulder, takes them to their home behind the Purple Hills.

One morning, just as usual, Old Mother West Wind turned the Merry Little Breezes out to play on the Green Meadows. Then she hurried away to fill the sails of the ships and blow them across the great ocean. The Merry Little Breezes hopped and skipped over the Green Meadows looking for some one to play with. It was then that one of them discovered something—something very dreadful.

It was a fire! Yes, Sir, it was a fire in the meadow grass! Some one had dropped a lighted match, and now little red flames were running through the grass in all directions. The Merry Little Breeze hastened to tell all the other Little Breezes and all

1

rushed over as fast as they could to see for themselves.

They saw how the little red flames were turning to smoke and ashes everything they touched, and how black and ugly, with nothing alive there, became that part of the Green Meadows where the little flames ran. It was dreadful! Then one of them noticed that the little red flames were running in the direction of Johnny Chuck's new house. Would the little red flames burn up Johnny Chuck, as they burned up the grass and the flowers?

"Hi!" cried the Merry Little Breeze, "We must warn Johnny Chuck and all the other little meadow people!"

So he caught up a capful of smoke and raced off as fast as he could go to Johnny Chuck's house. Then each of the Merry Little Breezes caught up a capful of smoke and started to warn one of the little meadow people or forest folks.

So pretty soon jolly, round, red Mr. Sun, looking down from the blue sky, saw Johnny Chuck, Jimmy Skunk, Peter Rabbit, Striped Chipmunk, Danny Meadow Mouse, Reddy Fox, Bobby Coon, Happy Jack Squirrel, Chatterer the Red Squirrel, Jumper the Hare and old Mr. Toad all hurrying as fast as they could to the Smiling Pool where live Billy Mink and Little Joe Otter and Jerry Muskrat and Spotty the Turtle and Great-Grandfather Frog. There they would be quite safe from the little red flames.

"Oh," gasped Johnny Chuck, puffing very hard, for you know he is round and fat and roly–poly and it was hard work for him to run, "what will become of my nice new house and what will there be left to eat?"

The Merry Little Breeze who had brought him the warning in a capful of smoke thought for a minute. Then he called all the other Little Breezes to him.

"We must get Farmer Brown's help or we will have no beautiful Green Meadows to play on," said the Merry Little Breeze.

So together they rushed back to where the little red flames had grown into great, angry, red flames that were licking up everything in their way. The Merry Little Breezes gathered a great cloud of smoke and, lifting all together, they carried it over and dropped it in Farmer Brown's dooryard. Then one of them blew a little of the smoke in at an open window, near which Farmer Brown was eating breakfast. Farmer Brown coughed and strangled and sprang from his chair.

"Phew!" cried Farmer Brown, "I smell smoke! There must be a fire on the meadows."

Then he shouted for his boy and for his hired man and the three, with shovels in their hands, started for the Green Meadows to try to put the fire out.

The Merry Little Breezes sighed with relief and followed to the fire. But when they saw how fierce and angry the red flames had become they knew that Farmer Brown and his boy and his hired man would not be able to put the fire out. Choking with smoke, they hurried over to tell the dreadful news to the little meadow people and forest folks gathered at the Smiling Pool.

"Chug-a-rum! Why don't you help put the fire out?" asked Grandfather Frog.

"We warned Farmer Brown and his boy and his hired man; what more can we do?" asked one of the Merry Little Breezes.

"Go find and drive up a rain cloud," replied Grandfather Frog.

"Splendid!" cried all the little meadow people and forest folks. "Hurry! hurry! Oh, do hurry!"

So the Merry Little Breezes scattered in all directions to hunt for a rain cloud.

"It is a good thing that Old Mother West Wind has such a big family," said Grandfather Frog, "for one of them is sure to find a wandering rain cloud somewhere."

Then all the little meadow people and forest folks sat down around the Smiling Pool to wait. They watched the smoke roll up until it hid the face of jolly, round, red Mr. Sun. Their hearts almost stood still with fear as they saw the fierce, angry, red flames leap into the air and climb tall trees on the edge of the Green Forest.

Splash! Something struck in the Smiling Pool right beside Grandfather Frog's big, green, lily-pad.

Spat! Something hit Johnny Chuck right on the end of his funny little, black nose.

They were drops of water.

"Hurrah!" cried Johnny Chuck, whirling about. Sure enough, they were drops of water—rain drops. And there, coming just as fast as the Merry Little Breezes could push it, and they were pushing very hard, very hard indeed, was a great, black, rain cloud, spilling down rain as it came.

When it was just over the fire, the great, black, rain cloud split wide open, and the water poured down so that the fierce, angry, red flames were drowned in a few minutes.

"Phew!" said Farmer Brown, mopping his face with his handkerchief, "that was warm work! That shower came up just in time and it is lucky it did."

But you know and I know and all the little meadow people and forest folks know that it wasn't luck at all, but the quick work and hard work of Old Mother West Wind's big family of Merry Little Breezes, which saved the Green Meadows. And this, too, is one reason why Peter Rabbit and Johnny Chuck and Bobby Coon and all the other little meadow and forest people love the Merry Little Breezes who play every day on the Green Meadows.

II
The Stranger in the Green Forest

OLD Mother West Wind, hurrying down from the Purple Hills with her Merry Little Breezes, discovered the newcomer in the Green Forest on the edge of the Green Meadows. Of course the Merry Little Breezes saw him, too, and as soon as Old Mother West Wind had turned them loose on the Green Meadows they started out to spread the news.

As they hurried along the Crooked Little Path up the hill, they met Reddy Fox.

"Oh, Reddy Fox," cried the Merry Little Breezes, so excited that all talked together, "there's a stranger in the Green Forest!"

Reddy Fox sat down and grinned at the Merry Little Breezes. The grin of Reddy Fox is not pleasant. It irritates and exasperates. It made the Merry Little Breezes feel very uncomfortable.

"You don't say so," drawled Reddy Fox. "Do you mean to say that you've just discovered him? Why, your news is so old that it is stale; it is no news at all. I thought you had something really new to tell me."

The Merry Little Breezes were disappointed. Their faces fell. They had thought it would be such

6

fun to carry the news through the Green Forest and over the Green Meadows, and now the very first one they met knew all about it.

"Who is he, Reddy Fox?" asked one of the Merry Little Breezes.

Reddy Fox pretended not to hear. "I must be going," said he, rising and stretching. "I have an engagement with Billy Mink down at the Smiling Pool."

Reddy Fox started down the Crooked Little Path while the Merry Little Breezes hurried up the Crooked Little Path to tell the news to Jimmy Skunk, who was looking for beetles for his breakfast.

Now Reddy Fox had not told the truth. He had known nothing whatever of the stranger in the Green Forest. In fact he had been as surprised as the Merry Little Breezes could have wished, but he would not show it. And he had told another untruth, for he had no intention of going down to the Smiling Pool. No, indeed! He just waited until the Merry Little Breezes were out of sight, then he slipped into the Green Forest to look for the stranger seen by the Merry Little Breezes.

Now Reddy Fox does nothing openly. Instead of walking through the Green Forest like a gentleman, he sneaked along under the bushes and crept from tree to tree, all the time looking for the stranger of whom the Merry Little Breezes had told him. All around through the Green Forest sneaked Reddy

Fox, but nothing of the stranger could he see. It didn't occur to him to look anywhere but on the ground.

"I don't believe there is a stranger here," said Reddy to himself.

Just then he noticed some scraps of bark around the foot of a tall maple. Looking up to see where it came from he saw—what do you think? Why, the stranger who had come to the Green Forest. Reddy Fox dodged back out of sight, for he wanted to find out all he could about the stranger before the stranger saw him.

Reddy sat down behind a big stump and rubbed his eyes. He could hardly believe what he saw. There at the top of the tall maple, stripping the branches of their bark and eating it, was the stranger, sure enough. He was big, much bigger than Reddy. Could he be a relative of Happy Jack Squirrel? He didn't look a bit, not the least little bit like Happy Jack. And he moved slowly, very slowly, indeed, while Happy Jack and his cousins move quickly. Reddy decided that the stranger could not be related to Happy Jack.

The longer Reddy looked the more he was puzzled. Also, Reddy began to feel just a little bit jealous. You see all the little meadow people and forest folks are afraid of Reddy Fox, but this stranger was so big that Reddy began to feel something very like fear in his own heart.

The Merry Little Breezes had told the news to

Jimmy Skunk and then hurried over the Green Meadows telling every one they met of the stranger in the Green Forest—Billy Mink, Little Joe Otter, Johnny Chuck, Peter Rabbit, Happy Jack Squirrel, Danny Meadow Mouse, Striped Chipmunk, old Mr. Toad, Great-Grandfather Frog, Sammy Jay, Blacky the Crow, and each as soon as he heard the news started for the Green Forest to welcome the newcomer. Even Great-Grandfather Frog left his beloved big, green lily-pad and started for the Green Forest.

So it was that when finally the stranger decided that he had eaten enough bark for his breakfast, and climbed slowly down the tall maple, he found all the little meadow people and forest folks sitting in a big circle waiting for him. The stranger was anything but handsome, but his size filled them with respect. The nearer he got to the ground the bigger he looked. Down he came, and Reddy Fox, noting how slow and clumsy in his movements was the stranger, decided that there was nothing to fear.

If the stranger was slow and clumsy in the tree, he was clumsier still on the ground. His eyes were small and dull. His coat was rough, long and almost black. His legs were short and stout. His tail was rather short and broad. Altogether he was anything but handsome. But when the little meadow people and forest folks saw his huge front teeth they regarded him with greater respect than ever, all but Reddy Fox.

Reddy strutted out in front of him. "Who are you?" he demanded. *See page 11.*

Reddy strutted out in front of him. "Who are you?" he demanded.

The stranger paid no attention to Reddy Fox.

"What business have you in our Green Forest?" demanded Reddy, showing all his teeth.

The stranger just grunted and appeared not to see Reddy Fox. Reddy swelled himself out until every hair stood on end and he looked twice as big as he really is. He strutted back and forth in front of the stranger.

"Don't you know that I'm afraid of nothing and nobody?" snarled Reddy Fox.

The stranger refused to give him so much as a glance. He just grunted and kept right on about his business. All the little meadow people and forest folks began to giggle and then to laugh. Reddy knew that they were laughing at him and he grew very angry, for no one likes to be laughed at, least of all Reddy Fox.

"You're a pig!" taunted Reddy. "You're afraid to fight. I bet you're afraid of Danny Meadow Mouse!"

Still the stranger just grunted and paid no further attention to Reddy Fox.

Now, with all his boasting Reddy Fox had kept at a safe distance from the stranger. Happy Jack Squirrel had noticed this. "If you're so brave, why don't you drive him out, Reddy Fox?" asked Happy Jack, skipping behind a tree. "You don't dare to!"

Reddy turned and glared at Happy Jack. "I'm not

afraid!" he shouted. "I'm not afraid of anything nor anybody!"

But though he spoke so bravely it was noticed that he went no nearer the stranger.

Now it happened that that morning Bowser the Hound took it into his head to take a walk in the Green Forest. Blacky the Crow, sitting on the tip-top of a big pine, was the first to see him coming. From pure love of mischief Blacky waited until Bowser was close to the circle around the stranger. Then he gave the alarm.

"Here's Bowser the Hound! Run!" screamed Blacky the Crow. Then he laughed so that he had to hold his sides to see the fright down below. Reddy Fox forgot that he was afraid of nothing and nobody. He was the first one out of sight, running so fast that his feet seemed hardly to touch the ground. Peter Rabbit turned a back somersault and suddenly remembered that he had important business down on the Green Meadows. Johnny Chuck dodged into a convenient hole. Billy Mink ran into a hollow tree. Striped Chipmunk hid in an old stump.

Happy Jack Squirrel climbed the nearest tree. In a twinkling the stranger was alone, facing Bowser the Hound.

Bowser stopped and looked at the stranger in sheer surprise. Then the hair on the back of his neck stood on end and he growled a deep, ugly growl. Still the stranger did not run. Bowser didn't know just what to make of it. Never before had he had such an experience. Could it be that the stranger was not afraid of him? Bowser walked around the stranger, growling fiercely. As he walked the stranger turned, so as always to face him. It was perplexing and very provoking. It really seemed as if the stranger had no fear of him.

"Bow, wow, wow!" cried Bowser the Hound in his deepest voice, and sprang at the stranger.

Then something happened, so surprising that Blacky the Crow lost his balance on the top of the pine where he was watching. The instant that Bowser sprang, the stranger rolled himself into a tight round ball and out of the long hair of his coat sprang hundreds of sharp little yellowish white barbed spears. The stranger looked for all the world like a huge black and yellow chestnut burr.

Bowser the Hound was as surprised as Blacky the Crow. He stopped short and his eyes looked as if they would pop out of his head. He looked so puzzled and so funny that Happy Jack Squirrel laughed aloud.

The stranger did not move. Bowser backed away and began to circle around again, sniffing and snuffing. Once in a while he barked. Still the stranger did not move. For all the sign of life he made he might in truth have been a giant chestnut burr.

Bowser sat down and looked at him. Then he walked around to the other side and sat down.

"What a queer thing," thought Bowser. "What a very queer thing."

Bowser took a step nearer. Then he took another step. Nothing happened.

Finally Bowser reached out, and with his nose gingerly touched the prickly ball. Slap! The stranger's tail had struck Bowser full in the face.

Bowser yelled with pain and rolled over and over on the ground. Sticking in his tender lips were a dozen sharp little spears, and claw and rub at them as he would, Bowser could not get them out. Every time he touched them he yelped with pain. Finally he gave it up and started for home with his tail between his legs like a whipped puppy, and with every step he yelped.

When he had disappeared and his yelps had died away in the distance, the stranger unrolled, the sharp little spears disappeared in the long hair of his coat and, just as if nothing at all had happened, the stranger walked slowly over to a tall maple and began to climb it.

And this is how Prickly Porky the Porcupine came to the Green Forest, and won the respect and admiration of all the little meadow people and forest folks, including Reddy Fox. Since that day no one has tried to meddle with Prickly Porky or his business.

III
How Prickly Porky Got His Quills

THE newcomer in the Green Forest was a source of great interest to the Merry Little Breezes. Ever since they had seen him turn himself into a huge prickly ball, like a giant chestnut burr, and with a slap of his tail send Bowser the Hound yelping home with his lips stuck full of little barbed spears, they had visited the Green Forest every day to watch Prickly Porky.

He was not very social. Indeed, he was not social at all, but attended strictly to his own business, which consisted chiefly of stripping bark from the trees and eating it. Never had the Merry Little Breezes seen such an appetite! Already that part of the Green Forest where he had chosen to live had many bare stark trees, killed that Prickly Porky the Porcupine might live. You see a tree cannot live without bark, and Prickly Porky had stripped them clean to fill his stomach.

But if Prickly Porky was not social he was not unfriendly. He seemed to enjoy having the Merry Little Breezes about, and did not in the least mind having them rumple up the long hair of his coat to feel the sharp little barbed spears underneath. Some of these were so loose that they dropped

15

out. Peter Rabbit's curiosity led him to examine some of these among bits of bark at the foot of a tree. Peter wished that he had left them alone. One of the sharp little barbs pierced his tender skin and Peter could not get it out. He had to ask Johnny Chuck to do it for him, and it had hurt dreadfully.

After that the little meadow people and forest folks held Prickly Porky in greater respect than ever and left him severely alone, which was just what he seemed to want.

One morning the Merry Little Breezes failed to find Prickly Porky in the Green Forest. Could he have left as mysteriously as he had come? They hurried down to the Smiling Pool to tell Great-Grandfather Frog. Bursting through the bulrushes on the edge of the Smiling Pool, they nearly upset Jerry Muskrat, who was sitting on an old log intently watching something out in the middle of the Smiling Pool. It was Prickly Porky. Some of the sharp little barbed spears were standing on end; altogether he was the queerest sight the Smiling Pool had seen for a long time.

He was swimming easily and you may be sure no one tried to bother him. Little Joe Otter and Billy Mink sat on the Big Rock and for once they had forgotten to play tricks. When Prickly Porky headed towards the Big Rock, Little Joe Otter suddenly remembered that he had business down the Laughing Brook, and Billy Mink recalled that

Mother Mink had forbidden him to play at the Smiling Pool. Prickly Porky had the Smiling Pool quite to himself.

When he had swum to his heart's content he climbed out, shook himself and slowly ambled up the Lone Little Path to the Green Forest. The Merry Little Breezes watched him out of sight. Then they danced over to the big green lily-pad on which sat Grandfather Frog. The Merry Little Breezes are great favorites with Grandfather Frog. As usual they brought him some foolish green flies. Grandfather Frog's eyes twinkled as he snapped up the last foolish green fly.

"Chug-a-rum!" said Grandfather Frog, "and now I suppose you want a story." And he folded his hands across his white and yellow waistcoat.

"If you please!" shouted the Merry Little Breezes. "If you please, do tell us how it is that Prickly Porky has spears on his back!"

Grandfather settled himself comfortably. "Chug-a-rum!" said he. "Once upon a time when the world was young, Mr. Porcupine, the grandfather a thousand times removed of Prickly Porky, whom you all know, lived in the Green Forest where old King Bear ruled. Mr. Porcupine was a slow clumsy fellow, just as his grandson a thousand times removed is to-day. He was so slow moving, and when he tried to hurry tumbled over himself so much, that he had hard work to get enough to eat. Always some one reached the berry patch before he did. The beetles and the bugs were so spry that seldom could he catch them. Hunger was in his stomach, and little else most of the time. Mr. Porcupine grew thin and thinner and still more thin. His long, shaggy coat looked twice too big for him. Because he was so hungry he could sleep little, and night as well as day he roamed the forest, thinking of nothing but his empty stomach, and looking for something to put in it. So he learned to see by night as well as by day.

"One day he could not find a single berry and not a beetle or a bug could he catch. He was so hungry that he sat down with his back against a big black birch, and clasping both hands over his lean stomach, he wept. There Sister South Wind found him, and her heart was moved to pity, for she knew that his wits were as slow as his body. Softly she stole up behind him.

"'Try the bark of the black birch; it's sweet and good,' whispered Sister South Wind. Then she hurried on her way.

"Mr. Porcupine still sat with his hands clasped over his lean stomach, for it took a long time for his slow wit to understand what Sister South Wind meant. 'Bark, bark, try bark,' said Mr. Porcupine over and over to himself. He rolled his dull little eyes up at the big black birch. 'I believe I will try it,' said Mr. Porcupine at last.

"Slowly he turned and began to gnaw the bark of the big black birch. It was tough, but it tasted good. Clumsily he began to climb, tearing off a mouthful of bark here and there as he climbed. The higher he got the tenderer and sweeter the bark became. Finally he reached the top of the tree, and there on the small branches the bark was so tender and so sweet that he ate and ate and ate until for the first time in many days Mr. Porcupine had a full stomach. That night he curled up in a hollow log and slept all the night through, dreaming of great forests of black birch and all he wanted to eat.

"The next day he hunted for and found another black birch, and climbing to the top, he ate and ate until his stomach was full. From that time on Mr. Porcupine ceased to hunt for berries or beetles or bugs. He grew stout and stouter. he filled his shaggy coat until it was so tight it threatened to burst.

"Now while Mr. Porcupine was so thin and lean he had no enemies, but when he grew stout and then fat, Mr. Panther and Mr. Fisher and Mr. Bobcat and even old King Bear began to cast longing eyes upon him, for times were hard and they were hungry. Mr. Porcupine began to grow afraid. By night he hid in hollow trees and by day he went abroad to eat only when he was sure that no one bigger than himself was about. And because he no longer dared to move about as before, he no longer depended upon the black birch alone, but learned to eat and to like all kinds of bark.

"One day he had made his breakfast on the bark

of a honey-locust. When he came down the tree he brought with him a strip of bark, and attached to it were some of the long thorns with which the honey-locust seeks to protect itself. When he reached the ground whom should he find waiting for him but Mr. Panther. Mr. Panther was very lean and very hungry, for hunting had been poor and the times were hard.

"'Good morning, Mr. Porcupine,' said Mr. Panther, with a wicked grin. 'How fat you are!'

"'Good morning, Mr. Panther,' said Mr. Porcupine politely, but his long hair stood on end with fright, as he looked into Mr. Panther's cruel yellow eyes.

"'I say, how fat you are,' said Mr. Panther, licking his chops and showing all his long teeth. 'What do you find to eat these hard times?'

"'Bark, Mr. Panther, just bark,' said Mr. Porcupine, while his teeth chattered with fear. 'It really is very nice and sweet. Won't you try a piece, Mr. Panther?' Mr. Porcupine held out the strip of locust bark which he had brought down the tree for his lunch.

"Now Mr. Panther had never tried bark, but he thought to himself that if it made Mr. Porcupine so fat it must be good. He would try the piece of bark first and eat Mr. Porcupine afterward. So he reached out and snapped up the strip of bark.

"Now the locust thorns were long and they were sharp. They pierced Mr. Panther's tender lips and his tongue. They struck in the roof of his mouth. Mr. Panther spat and yelled with pain and rage and clawed frantically at his mouth. He rolled over and over trying to get rid of the thorns. Mr. Porcupine didn't stay to watch him. For once in his life he hurried. By the time Mr. Panther was rid of the last thorn, Mr. Porcupine was nowhere to be seen. He was safely hidden inside a hollow log.

"Mr. Porcupine didn't sleep that night. He just lay and thought and thought and thought. The next morning, very early, before any one else was astir, he started out to call on old Mother Nature.

"'Good morning, Mr. Porcupine, what brings you out so early?' asked old Mother Nature.

"Mr. Porcupine bowed very low. 'If you please, Mother Nature, I want you to help me,' said he.

"Then he told her all about his meeting with Mr. Panther and how helpless he was when he met his enemies, and he begged her to give him stout claws and a big mouth full of long teeth that he might protect himself.

"Old Mother Nature thought a few minutes. 'Mr. Porcupine,' said she, 'you have always minded your own business. You do not know how to fight. If I should give you a big mouth full of long teeth you would not know how to use them. You move too slowly. Instead, I will give you a thousand little spears. They shall be hidden in the long hair of your coat and only when you are in danger shall you use them. Go back to the Green Forest, and the next time you meet Mr. Panther or Mr. Fisher or Mr. Bobcat or old King Bear roll yourself into a ball and the thousand little spears will protect you. Now go!'

"Mr. Porcupine thanked old Mother Nature and started back for the Green Forest. Once he stopped to smooth down his long, rough coat. Sure enough, there, under the long hair, he felt a thousand little spears. He went along happily until suddenly he met Mr. Panther. Yes, Sir, he met Mr. Panther.

"Mr. Panther was feeling very ugly, for his mouth was sore. He grinned wickedly when he saw Mr. Porcupine and stepped right out in front of him, all the time licking his lips. Mr. Porcupine trembled all over, but he remembered what old Mother Nature had told him. In a flash he had rolled up into a tight ball. Sure enough, the thousand little spears sprang out of his long coat, and he looked like a huge chestnut burr.

"Mr. Panther was so surprised he didn't know just what to do. He reached out a paw and touched Mr. Porcupine. Mr. Porcupine was nervous. He switched his tail around and it struck Mr. Panther's paw. Mr. Panther yelled, for there were spears on Mr. Porcupine's tail and they were worse than the locust thorns. He backed away hurriedly and limped off up the Lone Little Path, growling horribly. Mr. Porcupine waited until Mr. Panther was out of sight, then he unrolled, and slowly and happily he walked back to his home in the Green Forest.

"And since that long-ago day when the world was young, the Porcupines have feared nothing and have attended strictly to their own business. And that is how they happened to have a thousand little barbed spears, which are called quills," concluded Grandfather Frog.

The Merry Little Breezes drew a long breath. "Thank you, Grandfather Frog, thank you ever so much!" they cried all together. "We are going back now to tell Prickly Porky that we know all about his little spears and how he happens to have them."

But first they blew a dozen fat, foolish, green flies over to Grandfather Frog.

IV
Peter Rabbit's Egg Rolling

IT was spring. Drummer the Woodpecker was beating the long roll on the hollow limb of the old hickory, that all the world might know. Old Mother West Wind, hurrying down from the Purple Hills across the Green Meadows, stopped long enough to kiss the smiling little bluets that crowded along the Lone Little Path. All up and down the Laughing Brook were shy violets turning joyful faces up to jolly, round, red Mr. Sun. Johnny Chuck was sitting on his doorstep, stretching one short leg and then another, to get the kinks out, after his long, long winter sleep. Very beautiful, very beautiful indeed, were the Green Meadows, and very happy were all the little meadow people—all but Peter Rabbit, who sat at the top of the Crooked Little Path that winds down the hill. No, Sir, Peter Rabbit, happy-go-lucky Peter, who usually carries the lightest heart on the Green Meadows, was not happy. Indeed, he was very unhappy. As he sat there at the top of the Crooked Little Path and looked down on the Green Meadows, he saw nothing beautiful at all because, why, because his big soft eyes were full of tears. Splash! A big tear fell at his feet in the

24

Crooked Little Path. Splash! That was another tear. Splash! splash!

"My gracious! My gracious! What *is* the matter, Peter Rabbit?" asked a gruff voice close to one of Peter's long ears.

Peter jumped. Then he winked the tears back and looked around. There sat old Mr. Toad. He looked very solemn, very solemn indeed. He was wearing a shabby old suit, the very one he had slept in all winter. Peter forgot his troubles long enough to wonder if old Mr. Toad would swallow his old clothes when he got a new suit.

"What's the matter, Peter Rabbit, what's the matter?" repeated old Mr. Toad.

Peter looked a little foolish. He hesitated, coughed, looked this way and looked that way, hitched his trousers up, and then, why then he found his tongue and told old Mr. Toad all his troubles.

"You see," said Peter Rabbit, "it's almost Easter and I haven't found a single egg."

"An egg!" exclaimed old Mr. Toad. "Bless my stars! What do you want of an egg, Peter Rabbit? You don't eat eggs."

"I don't want just one egg, oh, no, no indeed! I want a lot of eggs," said Peter. "You see, Mr. Toad, I was going to have an Easter egg rolling, and here it is almost Easter and not an egg to be found!" Peter's eyes filled with tears again.

Old Mr. Toad rolled one eye up at jolly, round,

red Mr. Sun and winked. "Have you seen Mrs. Grouse and Mrs. Pheasant?" asked old Mr. Toad.

"Yes," said Peter Rabbit, "and they won't have any eggs until after Easter."

"Have you been to see Mrs. Quack?" asked old Mr. Toad.

"Yes," said Peter Rabbit, "and she says she can't spare a single one."

Old Mr. Toad looked very thoughtful. He scratched the tip of his nose with his left hind foot. Then he winked once more at jolly, round, red Mr. Sun. "Have you been to see Jimmy Skunk?" he inquired.

Peter Rabbit's big eyes opened very wide. "Jimmy Skunk!" he exclaimed. "Jimmy Skunk! What does Jimmy Skunk have to do with eggs?"

Old Mr. Toad chuckled deep down in his throat. He chuckled and chuckled until he shook all over.

"Jimmy Skunk knows more about eggs than all the other little meadow people put together," said old Mr. Toad. "You take my advice, Peter Rabbit, and ask Jimmy Skunk to help you get the eggs for your Easter egg rolling."

Then old Mr. Toad picked up his cane and started down the Crooked Little Path to the Green Meadows. There he found the Merry Little Breezes stealing kisses from the bashful little wind flowers. Old Mr. Toad puffed out his throat and pretended that he disapproved, disapproved very much indeed, but at the same time he rolled one eye up at jolly, round, red Mr. Sun and winked.

"Haven't you anything better to do than make bashful little flowers hang their heads?" asked old Mr. Toad gruffly.

The Merry Little Breezes stopped their dancing and gathered about old Mr. Toad. "What's the matter with you this morning, Mr. Toad?" asked one of them. "Do you want us to go find a breakfast for you?"

"No," replied old Mr. Toad sourly. "I am quite able to get breakfast for myself. But Peter Rabbit is up on the hill crying because he cannot find any eggs."

"Crying because he cannot find any eggs! Now what does Peter Rabbit want of eggs?" cried the Merry Little Breezes all together.

"Supposing you go ask him," replied old Mr. Toad tartly, once more picking up his cane and starting for the Smiling Pool to call on his cousin, Great-Grandfather Frog.

The Merry Little Breezes stared after him for a few minutes, then they started in a mad race up the Crooked Little Path to find Peter Rabbit. He wasn't at the top of the Crooked Little Path. They looked everywhere, but not so much as the tip of one of his long ears could they see. Finally they met him just coming away from Jimmy Skunk's house. Peter was hopping, skipping, jumping up in the air and kicking his long heels as only Peter can. There was no trace of tears in his big, soft eyes. Plainly Peter Rabbit was in good spirits, in the very best of spirits. When he saw the Merry Little Breezes he jumped twice as high as he had jumped before, then sat up very straight.

"Hello!" said Peter Rabbit.

"Hello yourself," replied the Merry Little Breezes. "Tell us what under the sun you want of eggs, Peter Rabbit, and we'll try to find some for you."

Peter's eyes sparkled. "I'm going to have an Easter egg rolling," said he, "but you needn't look for any eggs, for I am going to have all I want; Jimmy Skunk has promised to get them for me."

"What is an Easter egg rolling?" asked the Merry Little Breezes.

Peter looked very mysterious. "Wait and see," he replied. Then a sudden thought popped into his head. "Will you do something for me?" he asked.

Of course the Merry Little Breezes were delighted to do anything they could for Peter Rabbit, and told him so. So in a few minutes Peter had them scattering in every direction with invitations to all the little people of the Green Meadows and all the little folks of the Green Forest to attend his egg rolling on Easter morning.

Very, very early on Easter morning Old Mother West Wind hurried down from the Purple Hills and swept all the rain clouds out of the sky. Jolly, round, red Mr. Sun climbed up in the sky, smiling his broadest. All the little song birds sang their sweetest, and some who really cannot sing at all tried to just because they were so happy. Across the beautiful Green Meadows came all the little meadow people and forest folks to the smooth, grassy bank where the big hickory grows. Peter Rabbit was there waiting for them. He had brushed his clothes until you would hardly have known him. He felt very much excited and very important and very, very happy, for this was to be the very first egg rolling the Green Meadows had ever known, and it was all his very own.

Hidden behind the old hickory, tucked under pieces of bark, scattered among the bluets and wind flowers were big eggs, little eggs and middle-sized eggs, for Jimmy Skunk had been true to his promise. Where they came from Jimmy wouldn't tell. Perhaps if old Gray Goose and Mrs. Quack could have been there, they would have understood why it took so long to fill their nests. Perhaps if Farmer Brown's boy had happened along, he would have guessed why he had to hunt so long in the barn and under the henhouse to get enough eggs for breakfast. But Jimmy Skunk held his tongue and just smiled to see how happy Peter Rabbit was.

First came Peter's cousin, Jumper the Hare. Then up from the Smiling Pool came Jerry Muskrat, Little Joe Otter, Billy Mink, Grandfather Frog and Spotty the Turtle. Johnny Chuck, Danny Meadow Mouse, and old Mr. Toad came together. Of course Reddy Fox was on hand promptly. Striped Chipmunk came dancing out from the home no one has been able to find. Out from the Green Forest trotted Bobby Coon, Happy Jack Squirrel and Chatterer the Red Squirrel. Behind them shuffled Prickly Porky. Last of all came Jimmy Skunk, who never hurries, and Jimmy wore his very best suit of black and white. Up in the old hickory sat Blacky the Crow, Sammy Jay and Drummer the Woodpecker, to watch the fun.

When all had arrived, Peter Rabbit started them to hunting for the eggs. Everybody got in the way of everybody else. Even old Mr. Toad caught the excitement and hopped this way and hopped that way hunting for eggs. Danny Meadow Mouse found a goose egg bigger than himself and had to get help to bring it in. Bobby Coon stubbed his toes and fell down with an egg under each arm. Such a looking sight as he was! He had to go down to the Smiling Pool to wash.

By and by, when all the eggs had been found, Peter Rabbit sent a big goose egg rolling down the grassy bank and then raced after it to bring it back and roll it down again. In a few minutes the green grassy bank was covered with eggs—big eggs, little eggs, all kinds of eggs. Some were nearly round and rolled swiftly to the bottom. Some were sharp pointed at one end and rolled crookedly and sometimes turned end over end. A big egg knocked Johnny Chuck's legs from under him and, because Johnny Chuck is round and roly-poly, he just rolled over and over after the egg clear to the bottom of the green grassy bank. And it was such fun that he scrambled up and did it all over again.

Then Bobby Coon tried it. Pretty soon every one was trying it, even Reddy Fox, who seldom forgets his dignity. For once Blacky the Crow and Sammy Jay almost wished that they hadn't got wings, so that they might join in the fun.

But the greatest fun of all was when Prickly Porky decided that he, too, would join in the rolling. He tucked his head down in his vest and made himself into a perfectly round ball. Now when he did this, all his hidden spears stood out straight, until he looked like a great, giant, chestnut burr, and every one hurried to get out of his way. Over and over, faster and faster, he rolled down the green, grassy bank until he landed— where do you think? Why right in the midst of a lot of eggs that had been left when the other little people had scampered out of his way.

Now, having his head tucked into his vest, Prickly Porky couldn't see where he was going, so when he reached the bottom and hopped to his feet he didn't know what to make of the shout that went up from all the little meadow people. So foolish Prickly Porky lost his temper because he was being laughed at, and started off up the Lone Little Path to his home in the Green Forest. And what do you think? Why, stuck fast in a row on the spears on his back, Prickly Porky carried off six of Peter Rabbit's Easter eggs, and didn't know it.

V
How Johnny Chuck Ran Away

JOHNNY Chuck stood on the doorstep of his house and watched old Mrs. Chuck start down the Lone Little Path across the Green Meadows towards Farmer Brown's garden. She had her market basket on her arm, and Johnny knew that when she returned it would be full of the things he liked best. But not even the thought of these could chase away the frown that darkened Johnny Chuck's face. He had never been to Farmer Brown's garden and he had begged very hard to go that morning with old Mrs. Chuck. But she had said "No. It isn't safe for such a little chap as you." And when Mrs. Chuck said "No," Johnny knew that she meant it, and that it was of no use at all to beg.

So he stood with his hands in his pockets and scowled and scowled as he thought of old Mrs. Chuck's very last words: "Now, Johnny, don't you dare put a foot outside of the yard until I get back."

Pretty soon along came Peter Rabbit. Peter was trying to jump over his own shadow. When he saw Johnny Chuck he stopped abruptly. Then he looked up at the blue sky and winked at jolly, round, red Mr. Sun. "Looks mighty showery 'round here," he remarked to no one in particular.

Johnny Chuck smiled in spite of himself. Then he told Peter Rabbit how he had got to stay at home and mind the house and couldn't put his foot outside the yard. Now Peter hasn't had the best bringing up in the world, for his mother has such a big family that she is kept busy just getting them something to eat. So Peter has been allowed to bring himself up and do just about as he pleases.

"How long will your mother be gone?" asked Peter.

"Most all the morning," said Johnny Chuck mournfully.

Peter hopped a couple of steps nearer. "Say, Johnny," he whispered, "how is she going to know whether you stay in the yard all the time or not, so long as you are here when she gets home? I know where there's the dandiest sweet-clover patch. We can go over there and back easy before old Mrs. Chuck gets home, and she won't know anything about it. Come on!"

Johnny Chuck's mouth watered at the thought of the sweet-clover, but still he hesitated, for Johnny Chuck had been taught to mind.

"'Fraid cat! 'Fraid cat! Tied to your mother's apron strings!" jeered Peter Rabbit.

"I ain't either!" cried Johnny Chuck. And then, just to prove it, he thrust his hands into his pockets and swaggered out into the Lone Little Path.

"Where's your old clover patch?" asked he.

"I'll show you," said Peter Rabbit, and off he started, lipperty-lipperty-lip, so fast that Johnny Chuck lost his breath trying to make his short legs keep up. And all the time Johnny's conscience was pricking him.

Peter Rabbit left the Lone Little Path across the Green Meadows for some secret little paths of his own. His long legs took him over the ground very fast. Johnny Chuck, running behind him, grew tired and hot, for Johnny's legs are short and he is fat and roly-poly. At times all he could see was the white patch on the seat of Peter Rabbit's pants. He began to wish that he had minded old Mrs. Chuck and stayed at home. It was too late to go back now, for he didn't know the way.

"Wait up, Peter Rabbit!" he called.

Peter Rabbit just flirted his tail and ran faster.

"Please, please wait for me, Peter Rabbit," panted Johnny Chuck, and began to cry. Yes, Sir, he began to cry. You see he was so hot and tired, and then he was so afraid that he would lose sight of Peter Rabbit. If he did he would surely be lost, and then what should he do? The very thought made him run just a little faster.

Now Peter Rabbit is really one of the best-hearted little fellows in the world, just happy-go-lucky and careless. So when finally he looked back and saw Johnny Chuck way, way behind, with the tears running down his cheeks, and how hot and tired he

"Please, please wait for me, Peter Rabbit,"
panted Johnny Chuck. *See page 34.*

looked, Peter sat down and waited. Pretty soon Johnny Chuck came up, puffing and blowing, and threw himself flat on the ground.

"Please, Peter Rabbit, is it very much farther to the sweet-clover patch?" he panted, wiping his eyes with the backs of his hands.

"No," replied Peter Rabbit, "just a little way more. We'll rest here a few minutes and then I won't run so fast."

So Peter Rabbit and Johnny Chuck lay down in the grass to rest while Johnny Chuck recovered his breath. Every minute or two Peter would sit up very straight, prick up his long ears and look this way and look that way as if he expected to see something unusual. It made Johnny Chuck nervous.

"What do you keep doing that for, Peter Rabbit?" he asked.

"Oh, nothin'," replied Peter Rabbit. But he kept right on doing it just the same. Then suddenly, after one of these looks abroad, he crouched down very flat and whispered in Johnny Chuck's ear in great excitement.

"Old Whitetail is down here and he's headed this way. We'd better be moving," he said.

Johnny Chuck felt a chill of fear. "Who is Old Whitetail?" he asked, as he prepared to follow Peter Rabbit.

"Don't you know?" asked Peter in surprise. "Say, you are green! Why, he's Mr. Marsh Hawk, and if he once gets the chance he'll gobble you up, skin, bones and all. There's an old stone wall just a little way from here, and the sooner we get there the better!"

Peter Rabbit led the way, and if he had run fast before it was nothing to the way he ran now. A great fear made Johnny Chuck forget that he was tired, and he ran as he had never run before in all his short life. Just as he dived head-first into a hole between two big stones, a shadow swept over the grass and something sharp tore a gap in the seat of his pants and made him squeal with fright and pain. But he wriggled in beside Peter Rabbit and was safe, while Mr. Marsh Hawk flew off with a scream of rage and disappointment.

Johnny Chuck had never been so frightened in all his short life. He made himself as small as possible and crept as far as he could underneath a friendly stone in the old wall. His pants were torn and his leg smarted dreadfully where one of Mr. Marsh Hawk's cruel, sharp claws had scratched him. How he did wish that he had minded old Mrs. Chuck and stayed in his own yard, as she had told him to.

Peter Rabbit looked at the tear in Johnny Chuck's pants. "Pooh!" said Peter Rabbit, "don't mind a little thing like that."

"But I'm afraid to go home with my pants torn," said Johnny Chuck.

"Don't go home," replied Peter Rabbit. "I don't

unless I feel like it. You stay away a long time and then your mother will be so glad to see you that she won't ever think of the pants."

Johnny Chuck looked doubtful, but before he could say anything Peter Rabbit stuck his head out to see if the way was clear. It was, and Peter's long legs followed his head. "Come on, Johnny Chuck," he shouted. "I'm going over to the sweet-clover patch."

But Johnny Chuck was afraid. He was almost sure that Old Whitetail was waiting just outside to gobble him up. It was a long time before he would put so much as the tip of his wee black nose out. But without Peter Rabbit it grew lonesomer and lonesomer in under the old stone wall. Besides, he was afraid that he would lose Peter Rabbit, and then he would be lost indeed, for he didn't know the way home.

Finally Johnny Chuck ventured to peep out. There was jolly, round, red Mr. Sun smiling down just as if he was used to seeing little runaway chucks every day. Johnny looked and looked for Peter Rabbit, but it was a long time before he saw him, and when he did all he saw were Peter Rabbit's funny long ears above the tops of the waving grass, for Peter Rabbit was hidden in the sweet-clover patch, eating away for dear life.

It was only a little distance, but Johnny Chuck had had such a fright that he tried three times before he grew brave enough to scurry through the tall grass and join Peter Rabbit. My, how good that sweet-clover did taste! Johnny Chuck forgot all about Old Whitetail. He forgot all about his torn pants. He forgot that he had run away and didn't know the way home. He just ate and ate and ate until his stomach was so full he couldn't stuff another piece of sweet-clover into it.

Suddenly Peter Rabbit grabbed him by a sleeve and pulled him down flat.

"Sh-h-h," said Peter Rabbit, "don't move."

Johnny Chuck's heart almost stopped beating. What new danger could there be now? In a minute he heard a queer noise. Peeping between the stems of sweet-clover he saw—what do you think? Why, old Mrs. Chuck cutting sweet-clover to put in the basket of vegetables she was taking home from Farmer Brown's garden.

Johnny Chuck gave a great sigh of relief, but he kept very still for he did not want her to find him there after she had told him not to put foot outside his own dooryard. "You wait here," whispered Peter Rabbit, and crept off through the clover. Pretty soon Johnny Chuck saw Peter Rabbit steal up behind old Mrs. Chuck and pull four big lettuce leaves out of her basket.

VI
Peter Rabbit's Run for Life

"I WISH I hadn't run away," said Johnny Chuck dolefully, as he and Peter Rabbit peeped out from the sweet-clover patch and watched old Mrs. Chuck start for home with her market basket on her arm.

"You ought to think yourself lucky that your mother didn't find you here in the sweet-clover patch. If it hadn't been for me she would have," said Peter Rabbit.

Johnny Chuck's face grew longer and longer. His pants were torn, his leg was stiff and sore where old Mr. Marsh Hawk had scratched him that morning, but worse still his conscience pricked him. Yes, Sir, Johnny Chuck's conscience was pricking him hard, very hard indeed, because he had run away from home with Peter Rabbit after old Mrs. Chuck had told him not to leave the yard while she was away. Now he didn't know the way home.

"Peter Rabbit, I want to go home," said Johnny Chuck suddenly. "Isn't there a short cut so that I can get home before my mother does?"

"No, there isn't," said Peter Rabbit. "And if there was what good would it do you? Old Mrs.

Chuck would see that tear in your pants and then you'd catch it!"

"I don't care. Please won't you show me the way home, Peter Rabbit?" begged Johnny Chuck.

Peter Rabbit yawned lazily as he replied: "What's the use of going now? You'll catch it anyway, so you might as well stay and have all the fun you can. Say, I know a dandy old house up on the hill. Jimmy Skunk used to live there, but no one lives in it now. Let's go up and see it. It's a dandy place."

Now right down in his heart Johnny Chuck knew that he ought to go home, but he couldn't go unless Peter Rabbit would show him the way, and then he did want to see that old house. Perhaps Peter Rabbit was right (in his heart he knew that he wasn't) and he had better have all the fun he could. So Johnny Chuck followed Peter Rabbit up the hill to the old house of Jimmy Skunk.

Cobwebs covered the doorway. Johnny Chuck was going to brush them away, but Peter Rabbit stopped him. "Let's see if there isn't a back door," said he. "Then we can use that, and if Bowser the Hound or Farmer Brown's boy comes along and finds this door they'll think no one ever lives here any more and you'll be safer than if you were right in your own home."

So they hunted and hunted, and by and by Johnny Chuck found the back door way off at one side and cunningly hidden under a tangle of grass. Inside was a long dark hall and at the end of that a nice big room. It was very dirty, and Johnny Chuck, who is very neat, at once began to clean house and soon had it spick and span. Suddenly they heard a voice outside the front door.

"Doesn't look as if anybody lives here, but seems as if I smell young rabbit and—yes, I'm sure I smell young chuck, too. Guess I'll have a look inside."

"It's old Granny Fox," whispered Peter Rabbit, trembling with fright.

Then Peter Rabbit did a very brave thing. He remembered that Johnny Chuck could not run very fast and that if it hadn't been for him, Johnny Chuck would be safe at home. "You stay right here," whispered Peter Rabbit. Then he slipped out the back door. Half-way down the hill he stopped and shouted:

"Old Granny Fox
Is slower than an ox!"

Then he started for the old brier patch as fast as his long legs could take him, and after him ran Granny Fox.

Peter Rabbit was running for his life. There was no doubt about it. Right behind him, grinding her long white teeth, her eyes snapping, ran old Granny Fox. Peter Rabbit did not like to think what would happen to him if she should catch him.

Peter Rabbit was used to running for his life. He had to do it at least once every day. But usually he was near a safe hiding place and he rather enjoyed the excitement. This time, however, the only place of safety he could think of was the friendly old brier patch, and that was a long way off.

Back at the old house on the hill, where Granny Fox had discovered Peter Rabbit, was little Johnny Chuck, trembling with fright. He crept to the back door of the old house to watch. He saw Granny Fox getting nearer and nearer to Peter Rabbit.

"Oh, dear! Oh, dear! She'll catch Peter Rabbit! She'll catch Peter Rabbit!" wailed Johnny Chuck, wringing his hands in despair.

It certainly looked as if Granny Fox would. She was right at Peter Rabbit's heels. Poor, happy-go-lucky, little Peter Rabbit! Two more jumps and Granny Fox would have him! Johnny Chuck shut his eyes tight, for he didn't want to see.

But Peter Rabbit had no intention of being caught so easily. While he had seemed to be running his very hardest, really he was not. And all the time he was watching Granny Fox, for Peter Rabbit's big eyes are so placed that he can see behind him without turning his head. So he knew when Granny Fox was near enough to catch him in one more jump. Then Peter Rabbit dodged. Yes, Sir, Peter Rabbit dodged like a flash, and away he went in another direction lipperty-lippety-lip, as fast as he could go.

Old Granny Fox had been so sure that in another minute she would have tender young rabbit for her dinner that she had begun to smile and her mouth actually watered. She did not see where she was going. All she saw was the white patch on the seat of Peter Rabbit's trousers bobbing up and down right in front of her nose.

When Peter Rabbit dodged, something surprising happened. Johnny Chuck, who had opened his eyes to see if all was over, jumped up and shouted for joy, and did a funny little dance in the doorway of the old house on the hill. Peter had dodged right in front of a wire fence, a fence with ugly, sharp barbs, and right smack into it ran Granny Fox! It scratched her face and tore her bright red cloak. It threw her back flat on the ground, with all the wind knocked out of her body.

When finally she had gotten her breath and scrambled to her feet, Peter Rabbit was almost over to the friendly old brier patch. He stopped and sat up very straight. Then he put his hands on his hips and shouted:

"Run, Granny, run!
Here comes a man who's got a gun!"

Granny Fox started nervously and looked this way and looked that way. There was no one in sight. Then she shook a fist at Peter Rabbit and started to limp off home.

Johnny Chuck gave a great sigh of relief. "My," said he, "I wish I was as smart as Peter Rabbit!"

"You will be if you live long enough," said a voice right behind him. It was old Mr. Toad.

Mr. Toad and Johnny Chuck sat in the doorway of the old house on the hill and watched old Granny Fox limp off home. "I wonder what it would seem like not to be afraid of anything in the whole world," said Johnny Chuck.

"People who mind their own business and don't get into mischief don't need to be afraid of anything," said Mr. Toad.

Johnny Chuck remembered how safe he had always felt at home with old Mrs. Chuck and how many times and how badly he had been frightened since he ran away that morning. "I guess perhaps you are right, Mr. Toad," said Johnny Chuck doubtfully.

"Of course I'm right," replied Mr. Toad. "Of course I'm right. Look at me; I attend strictly to my own affairs and no one ever bothers me."

"That's because you are so homely that no one wants you for a dinner when he can find anything else," said Peter Rabbit, who had come up from the friendly old brier patch.

"Better be homely than to need eyes in the back of my head to keep my skin whole," retorted Mr. Toad. "Now I don't know what it is to be afraid."

"Not of old Granny Fox?" asked Johnny Chuck.

"No," said Mr. Toad.

"Nor Bowser the Hound?"

"No," said Mr. Toad. "He's a friend of mine." Then Mr. Toad swelled himself up very big. "I'm not afraid of anything under the sun," boasted Mr. Toad.

Peter Rabbit looked at Johnny Chuck and slowly winked one eye. "I guess I'll go up the hill and have a look around," said Peter Rabbit, hitching up his trousers. So Peter Rabbit went off up the hill, while Mr. Toad smoothed down his dingy white waistcoat and told Johnny Chuck what a foolish thing fear is.

By and by there was a queer rustling in the grass back of them. Mr. Toad hopped around awkwardly. "What was that?" he whispered.

"Just the wind in the grass, I guess," said Johnny Chuck.

For a while all was still and Mr. Toad settled himself comfortably and began to talk once more. "No, Sir," said Mr. Toad, "I'm not afraid of anything."

Just then there was another rustle in the grass, a little nearer than before. Mr. Toad certainly was nervous. He stretched up on the tips of his toes and looked in the direction of the sound. Then Mr. Toad turned pale. Yes, Sir, Mr. Toad actually turned pale! His big, bulging eyes looked as if they would pop out of his head.

"I—I must be going," said Mr. Toad hastily. "I quite forgot an important engagement down on the Green Meadows. If Mr. Blacksnake should happen to call, don't mention that you have seen me, will you, Johnny Chuck?"

Johnny Chuck looked over in the grass. Something long and slim and black was wriggling through it. When he turned about again, Mr. Toad was half-way down the hill, going with such big hops that three times he fell flat on his face, and when he picked himself up he didn't even stop to brush off his clothes.

"I wonder what it seems like not to be afraid of anything in the world?" said a voice right behind Johnny Chuck.

There stood Peter Rabbit laughing so that he had to hold his sides, and in one hand was the end of an old leather strap which he had fooled Mr. Toad into thinking was Mr. Blacksnake.

VII
A Joker Fooled

PETER Rabbit and Johnny Chuck sat in the door-way of Jimmy Skunk's deserted old house on the hill and looked down across the Green Meadows. Every few minutes Peter Rabbit would chuckle as he thought of how he had fooled Mr. Toad into thinking that an old leather strap was Mr. Blacksnake.

"Is Mr. Blacksnake so very dangerous?" asked Johnny Chuck, who had seen very little of the world.

"Not for you or me," replied Peter Rabbit, "because we've grown too big for him to swallow. But he would like nothing better than to catch Mr. Toad for his dinner. But if you ever meet Mr. Blacksnake, be polite to him. He is very quick tempered, is Mr. Blacksnake, but if you don't bother him he'll not bother you. My goodness, I wonder what's going on down there in the alders!"

Johnny Chuck looked over to the alder thicket. He saw Sammy Jay, Blacky the Crow and Mrs. Redwing sitting in the alders. They were calling back and forth, apparently very much excited. Peter Rabbit looked this way and that way to see if the coast was clear.

"Come on, Johnny Chuck, let's go down and see what the trouble is," said he, for you know Peter Rabbit has a great deal of curiosity.

So down to the alder thicket skipped Peter Rabbit and Johnny Chuck as fast as they could go. Halfway there they were joined by Danny Meadow Mouse, for he too had heard the fuss and wanted to know what it all meant.

"What's the matter?" asked Peter Rabbit of Sammy Jay, but Sammy was too excited to answer and simply pointed down into the middle of the alder thicket. So the three of them, one behind the other, very softly crept in among the alders. A great commotion was going on among the dead leaves. Danny Meadow Mouse gave one look, then he turned as pale as did Mr. Toad when Peter Rabbit fooled him with the old leather strap. "This is no place for me!" exclaimed Danny Meadow Mouse, and started for home as fast as he could run.

Partly under an old log lay Mr. Blacksnake. There seemed to be something the matter with him. He looked sick, and threshed and struggled till he made the leaves fly. Sammy Jay and Blacky the Crow and Mrs. Redwing called all sorts of insulting things to him, but he paid no attention to them. Once Mrs. Redwing darted down and pecked him sharply. But Mr. Blacksnake seemed quite helpless.

"What's the matter with him?" asked Johnny Chuck in a whisper.

"Nothing. Wait and you'll see. Sammy Jay and Mrs. Redwing better watch out or they'll be sorry," replied Peter Rabbit.

Just then Mr. Blacksnake wedged his head in under the old log and began to push and wriggle harder than ever. Then Johnny Chuck gasped. Mr. Blacksnake was crawling out of his clothes! Yes, Sir, his old suit was coming off wrong side out, just like a glove, and underneath he wore a splendid new suit of shiny black!

"It's time for us to be moving," whispered Peter Rabbit. "After Mr. Blacksnake has changed his clothes he is pretty short tempered. Just hear him hiss at Mrs. Redwing and Sammy Jay!"

They tiptoed out of the alder thicket and started back for the old house on the hill. Peter Rabbit suddenly giggled out loud. "To-morrow," said Peter Rabbit "we'll come back and get Mr. Blacksnake's old suit and have some fun with Danny Meadow Mouse."

The next morning Danny Meadow Mouse sat on his doorstep nodding. He was dreaming that his tail was long like the tails of all his cousins. One of Old Mother West Wind's Merry Little Breezes stole up and whispered in his ear. Danny Meadow Mouse was awake, wide awake in an instant. "So Peter Rabbit is going to play a joke on me and scare me into fits!" said Danny Meadow Mouse.

"Yes," said the Merry Little Breeze, "for I overheard him telling Johnny Chuck all about it."

Danny Meadow Mouse began to laugh softly to himself. "Will you do something for me?" he asked the Merry Little Breeze.

"Sure," replied the Merry Little Breeze.

"Then go find Cresty the Fly-catcher and tell him that I want to see him," said Danny Meadow Mouse.

The Merry Little Breeze hurried away, and pretty soon back he came with Cresty the Fly-catcher.

Now all this time Peter Rabbit had been very busy planning his joke on Danny Meadow Mouse. He and Johnny Chuck had gone down to the alder thicket, where they had seen Mr. Blacksnake change his clothes, and they had found his old suit just as he had left it.

"We'll take this up and stretch it out behind a big tussock of grass near the home of Danny Meadow Mouse," chuckled Peter Rabbit. "Then I'll invite Danny Meadow Mouse to take a walk, and when we come by the tussock of grass he will think he sees Mr. Blacksnake himself all ready to swallow him. Then we'll see some fun."

So they carried Mr. Blacksnake's old suit of clothes and hid it behind the big tussock of grass, and arranged it to look as much like Mr. Blacksnake as they could. Then Johnny Chuck went back to the old house on the hill to watch the fun, while Peter Rabbit went to call on Danny Meadow Mouse.

"Good morning, Peter Rabbit," said Danny Meadow Mouse politely.

"Good morning, Danny Meadow Mouse," replied Peter Rabbit. "Don't you want to take a walk with me this fine morning?"

"I'll be delighted to go," said Danny Meadow Mouse, reaching for his hat.

So they started out to walk and presently they came to the big tussock of grass.

Peter Rabbit stopped. "Excuse me, while I tie up my shoe. You go ahead and I'll join you in a minute," said Peter Rabbit.

So Danny Meadow Mouse went ahead. As soon as his back was turned Peter Rabbit clapped both hands over his mouth to keep from laughing, for you see he expected to see Danny Meadow Mouse come flying back in great fright the minute he turned the big tussock and saw Mr. Blacksnake's old suit.

Peter Rabbit waited and waited, but no Danny Meadow Mouse. What did it mean? Peter stopped laughing and peeped around the big tussock. There sat Danny Meadow Mouse with both hands clapped over his mouth, and laughing till the tears rolled down his cheeks, and Mr. Blacksnake's old suit was nowhere to be seen.

"He laughs best who laughs last," said Danny Meadow Mouse to himself, late that afternoon, as he sat on his doorstep and chuckled softly.

When he had first heard from a Merry Little Breeze that Peter Rabbit and Johnny Chuck were planning to play a joke on him and scare him into fits with a suit of Mr. Blacksnake's old clothes, he had tried very hard to think of some way to turn the joke on the jokers. Then he had remembered Cresty the Fly-catcher and had sent for him.

Now Cresty the Fly-catcher is a handsome fellow. In fact he is quite the gentleman, and does not look at all like one who would be at all interested in any one's old clothes. But he is. He is never satisfied until he has lined the hollow in the old apple-tree, which is his home, with the old clothes of Mr. Snake.

So when Danny Meadow Mouse sent for him and whispered in his ear Cresty the Fly-catcher smiled broadly and winked knowingly. "I certainly will be there, Danny Meadow Mouse, I certainly will be there," said he. And he was there. He had hidden in a tree close by the big tussock of grass, behind which Peter Rabbit had planned to place Mr. Blacksnake's old suit so as to scare Danny Meadow Mouse. His eyes had sparkled when he saw what a fine big suit it was. "My, but this will save me a lot of trouble," said he to himself. "It's the finest old suit I've ever seen."

The minute Peter Rabbit and Johnny Chuck had turned their backs down dropped Cresty the Fly-catcher, picked up Mr. Blacksnake's old suit, and taking it with him, once more hid in the tree. Presently back came Peter Rabbit with Danny Meadow Mouse. You know what had happened then.

Cresty the Fly-catcher had nearly dropped his prize, it tickled him so to see Peter Rabbit on one side of the big tussock laughing fit to kill himself at the scare he thought Danny Meadow Mouse would get when he first saw Mr. Blacksnake's old suit, and on the other side of the big tussock Danny Meadow Mouse laughing fit to kill himself over the surprise Peter Rabbit would get when he found that Mr. Blacksnake's old clothes had disappeared.

Pretty soon Peter Rabbit had stopped laughing and peeped around the big tussock. There sat Danny Meadow Mouse laughing fit to kill himself, but not a trace of the old suit which was to have given him such a scare. Peter couldn't believe his own eyes, for he had left it there not three minutes before. Of course it wouldn't do to say anything about it, so he had hurried around the big tussock as if he was merely trying to catch up.

"What are you laughing at, Danny Meadow Mouse?" asked Peter Rabbit.

"I was thinking what a joke it would be if we could only find an old suit of Mr. Blacksnake's and fool old Mr. Toad into thinking that it was Mr. Blacksnake himself," replied Danny Meadow Mouse. "What are you looking for, Peter Rabbit? Have you lost something?"

"No," said Peter Rabbit. "I thought I heard footsteps, and I was looking to see if it could be Reddy Fox creeping through the grass."

Danny Meadow Mouse had stopped laughing.

"Excuse me, Peter Rabbit," said he hurriedly, "I've just remembered an important engagement." And off he started for home as fast as he could go.

And to this day Peter Rabbit doesn't know what became of Mr. Blacksnake's old clothes.

VIII

The Fuss in the Big Pine

PETER Rabbit hopped down the Crooked Little Path to the Lone Little Path and down the Lone Little Path to the home of Johnny Chuck. Johnny Chuck sat on his doorstep dreaming. They were very pleasant dreams, very pleasant dreams indeed. They were such pleasant dreams that for once Johnny Chuck forgot to put his funny little ears on guard. So Johnny Chuck sat on his doorstep dreaming and heard nothing.

Lipperty-lipperty-lip down the Lone Little Path came Peter Rabbit. He saw Johnny Chuck and he stopped long enough to pluck a long stem of grass. Then very, very softly he stole up behind Johnny Chuck. Reaching out with the long stem of grass, he tickled one of Johnny Chuck's ears.

Johnny Chuck slapped at his ear with a little black hand, for he thought a fly was bothering him, just as Peter Rabbit meant that he should. Peter tickled the other ear. Johnny Chuck shook his head and slapped at this with the other little black hand. Peter almost giggled. He sat still a few minutes, then tickled Johnny Chuck again. Johnny slapped three or four times at the imaginary fly. This time

Peter clapped both hands over his mouth to keep from laughing.

Once more he tickled Johnny Chuck. This time Johnny jumped clear off his doorstep. Peter laughed before he could clap his hands over his mouth. Of course Johnny Chuck heard him and whirled about. When he saw Peter Rabbit and the long stem of grass he laughed, too.

"Hello, Peter Rabbit! You fooled me that time. Where'd you come from?" asked Johnny Chuck.

"Down the Lone Little Path from the Crooked Little Path and down the Crooked Little Path from the top of the Hill," replied Peter Rabbit.

Then they sat down side by side on Johnny Chuck's doorstep to watch Reddy Fox hunting for his dinner on the Green Meadows.

Pretty soon they heard Blacky the Crow cawing very loudly. They could see him on the tip-top of a big pine in the Green Forest on the edge of the Green Meadows.

"Caw, caw, caw," shouted Blacky the Crow, at the top of his lungs.

In a few minutes they saw all of Blacky's aunts and uncles and cousins flying over to join Blacky at the big pine in the midst of the Green Forest. Soon there was a big crowd of crows around the big pine, all talking at once. Such a racket! Such a dreadful racket! Every few minutes one of them would fly into the big pine and yell at the top of his lungs. Then all would caw together. Another would fly into the big pine and they would do it all over again.

Peter Rabbit began to get interested, for you know Peter has a very great deal of curiosity.

"Now I wonder what Blacky the Crow and his aunts and his uncles and his cousins are making such a fuss about," said Peter Rabbit.

"I'm sure I don't know," replied Johnny Chuck. "They seem to be having a good time, anyway. My gracious, how noisy they are!"

Just then along came Sammy Jay, who is, as you know, first cousin to Blacky the Crow. He was coming from the direction of the big pine.

"Sammy! Oh, Sammy Jay! What is all that fuss about over in the big pine?" shouted Peter Rabbit.

Sammy Jay stopped and carefully brushed his handsome blue coat, for Sammy Jay is something of a dandy. He appeared not to have heard Peter Rabbit.

"Sammy Jay, are you deaf?" inquired Peter Rabbit.

Now of course Sammy Jay had seen Peter Rabbit and Johnny Chuck all the time, but he looked up as if very much surprised to find them there.

"Oh, hello, Peter Rabbit!" said Sammy Jay. "Did you speak to me?"

"No, oh, no," replied Peter Rabbit in disgust. "I was talking to myself, just thinking out loud. I was wondering how many nuts a Jay could steal if he had the chance."

Johnny Chuck chuckled and Sammy Jay looked foolish. He couldn't find a word to say, for he knew that all the little meadow people knew how he once was caught stealing Happy Jack's store of nuts.

"I asked what all that fuss over in the big pine is about," continued Peter Rabbit.

"Oh," said Sammy Jay, "my cousin, Blacky the Crow, found Hooty the Owl asleep over there, and now he and his aunts and his uncles and his cousins are having no end of fun with him. You know Hooty the Owl cannot see in the daytime very well, and they can do almost anything to him that they want to. It's great sport."

"I don't see any sport in making other people uncomfortable," said Johnny Chuck.

"Nor I," said Peter Rabbit. "I'd be ashamed to own a cousin like Blacky the Crow. I like people who mind their own affairs and leave other people alone."

Sammy Jay ran out his tongue at Peter Rabbit.

"You are a nice one to talk about minding other folk's affairs!" jeered Sammy Jay.

> "Peter Rabbit's ears are long;
>   I wonder why! I wonder why!
> Because to hear what others say
>   He's bound to try! he's bound to try."

It was Peter Rabbit's turn to look discomfited.

"Anyway, I don't try to bully and torment others and I don't steal," he retorted.

> "Sammy Jay's a handsome chap
> And wears a coat of blue. ·
> I wonder if it's really his
> Or if he stole *that,* too."

Just then Johnny Chuck's sharp eyes caught sight of something stealing along the edge of the Green Meadows toward the Green Forest and the big pine.

"There's Farmer Brown's boy with a gun," cried Johnny Chuck. "There's going to be trouble at the big pine if Blacky the Crow doesn't watch out. That's what comes of being so noisy."

Peter Rabbit and Sammy Jay stopped quarreling to look. Sure enough, there was Farmer Brown's boy with his gun. He had heard Blacky the Crow and his aunts and his uncles and his cousins and he had hurried to get his gun, hoping to take them by surprise.

But Blacky the Crow has sharp eyes, too. Indeed, there are none sharper. Then, too, he is a mischief-maker. Mischief-makers are always on the watch lest they get caught in their mischief. So Blacky the Crow, sitting on the tip-top of the big pine, kept one eye out for trouble while he enjoyed the torment-ing of Hooty the Owl by his aunts and his uncles and his cousins. He had seen Farmer Brown's boy even before Johnny Chuck had. But he couldn't bear to spoil the fun of tormenting Hooty the Owl, so he waited just as long as he dared. Then he gave the signal.

"Caw, caw, caw, caw!" shouted Blacky at the top of his lungs.

"Caw, caw, caw, caw!" replied all his aunts and uncles and cousins, rising into the air in a black cloud. Then, with Blacky in the lead, they flew over on to the Green Meadows, laughing and talking noisily as they went.

Farmer Brown's boy did not try to follow them, for he knew that it was of not the least bit of use. But he was curious to learn what the crows had been making such a fuss about, so he kept on towards the big pine.

Johnny Chuck watched him go. Suddenly he remembered Hooty the Owl, and that Hooty cannot see well in the daytime. Very likely Hooty would think that the crows had become tired of tormenting him and had gone off of their own accord. Farmer Brown's boy would find him there and then—Johnny Chuck shuddered as he thought of what might happen to Hooty the Owl.

"Run, Peter Rabbit, run as fast as you can down on the Green Meadows where the Merry Little Breezes are at play and send one of them to tell Hooty the Owl that Farmer Brown's boy is coming with a gun to the big pine! Hurry, Peter, hurry!" cried Johnny Chuck.

Peter did not need to be told twice. He saw the

danger of Hooty the Owl, and he started down the Lone Little Path on to the Green Meadows so fast that in a few minutes all Johnny Chuck and Sammy Jay could see of him was a little spot of white, which was the patch on the seat of Peter's pants, bobbing through the grass on the Green Meadows.

Johnny Chuck would have gone himself, but he is round and fat and roly-poly and cannot run fast, while Peter Rabbit's legs are long and meant for running. In a few minutes Johnny Chuck saw one of the Merry Little Breezes start for the big pine as fast as he could go. Johnny gave a great sigh of relief.

Farmer Brown's boy kept on to the big pine. When he got there he found no one there, for Hooty the Owl had heeded the warning of the Merry Little Breeze and had flown into the deepest, darkest part of the Green Forest, where not even the sharp eyes of Blacky the Crow were likely to find him.

And back on his doorstep Johnny Chuck chuckled to himself, for he was happy, was Johnny Chuck, happy because he possessed the best thing in the world, which is contentment.

And this is all I am going to tell you about the fuss in the big pine.

IX
Johnny Chuck Finds a Use for His Back Door

JOHNNY Chuck sat in his doorway looking over the Green Meadows. He felt very fine. He had had a good breakfast in the sweet-clover patch. He had had a good nap on his own doorstep. By and by he saw the Merry Little Breezes of old Mother West Wind hurrying in his direction. They seemed in a very great hurry. They didn't stop to kiss the buttercups or tease the daisies. Johnny pricked up his small ears and watched them hurry up the hill.

"Good morning, Johnny Chuck," panted the first Merry Little Breeze to reach him, "have you heard the news?"

"What news," asked Johnny Chuck.

"The news about old Mother Chuck," replied the Merry Little Breezes.

Johnny shook his head.

"No," said he. "What is it?"

The Merry Little Breezes grew very, very sober.

"It is bad news," they replied.

"What is it? Tell me quick!" begged Johnny.

Just then Reddy Fox came hopping and skipping down the Lone Little Path.

"Hi, Johnny Chuck, have you heard the news?"

"No," said Johnny Chuck, "do tell me quick!"

Reddy Fox grinned maliciously, for Reddy likes to torment others. "It's about old Mrs. Chuck," said Reddy.

"I know that already," replied Johnny, "but, please, what is it?"

"Farmer Brown's boy has caught old Mrs. Chuck, and now I wouldn't wonder but what he will come up here and catch you," replied Reddy, turning a somersault.

Johnny Chuck grew pale. He had not seen Mother Chuck to speak to since he ran away from home. Now he was glad that he had run away, and yet sorry, oh, so sorry that anything had happened to Mrs. Chuck. Two big tears came into his eyes and ran down his funny little black nose. The Merry Little Breezes saw this, and one of them hurried over and whispered in Johnny Chuck's ear.

"Don't cry, Johnny Chuck," whispered the Merry Little Breeze. "Old Mother Chuck got away, and Farmer Brown's boy is still wondering how she did it."

Johnny's heart gave a great throb of relief. "I don't believe that Farmer Brown's boy will catch me," said Johnny Chuck, "for my house has two back doors."

Johnny Chuck awoke very early the next morning. He stretched and yawned and then just lay quietly enjoying himself for a few minutes. His bedchamber, way down underground, was snug and warm and very, very comfortable.

By and by, Johnny Chuck heard a noise up by his front door.

"I wonder what is going on out there," said Johnny Chuck to himself, and jumping up, he tiptoed softly up the long hall until he had almost reached his doorway. Then he heard a voice which he had heard before, and it made little shivers run all over him. It was the voice of Granny Fox.

"So this is where that fat little Chuck has made his home," said Granny Fox.

"Yes," replied another voice, "this is where Johnny Chuck lives, for I saw him here yesterday."

Johnny pricked up his ears, for that was the voice of Reddy Fox.

"Do you think he is in here now?" inquired Granny Fox.

"I am sure of it," replied Reddy, "for I have been watching ever since jolly, round, red Mr. Sun threw his nightcap off this morning, and Johnny Chuck has not put his nose out yet."

"Good," said Granny Fox, "I think fat Chuck will taste good for breakfast."

Johnny felt the cold shivers run over him again as he heard Granny Fox and Reddy Fox smack their lips. Then Granny Fox spoke again:

"You lie down behind that bunch of grass over there, Reddy, and I will lie down behind the old apple-tree. When he comes out, you just jump into his doorway and I will catch him before he can say Jack Robinson."

Johnny waited and listened and listened, but all was as still as still could be. Then Johnny Chuck tiptoed back along the hall to his bedroom and sat down to think. He felt sure that Granny Fox and Reddy were waiting for him, just as he had heard them plan.

"However am I going to know when they leave?" said Johnny Chuck to himself. Then he remembered the back doors which he had taken such care to make, and which Peter Rabbit had laughed at him for taking the trouble to make. He had hidden one so cunningly in the long grass and had so carefully removed all sand from around it that he felt quite sure that no one had found it.

Very softly Johnny Chuck crept along the back passageway. Very, very cautiously he stuck his little black nose out the doorway and sniffed. Yes, he could smell foxes, but he knew that they were not at his back door. Little by little he crept out until he could peep through the grass. There lay Reddy Fox behind a big clump of grass, his eyes fixed on Johnny Chuck's front door, and there behind the apple-tree lay Granny Fox taking her ease, but all ready to jump when Reddy should give the word. Johnny Chuck almost giggled out loud as he saw how eagerly Reddy Fox was watching for him. Then Johnny Chuck had an idea that made him giggle harder. His black eyes snapped and he chuckled to himself.

Pretty soon along came Bumble the Bee, looking

for honey. He came bustling and humming through the tall grass and settled on a dandelion right on the doorstep of Johnny Chuck's back door.

"Good morning," grumbled Bumble the Bee.

Johnny put a hand on his lips and beckoned Bumble to come inside.

Now Bumble the Bee is a gruff and rough fellow, but he is a good fellow, too, when you know him. Johnny Chuck had many times told him of places where the flowers grew thick and sweet, so when Johnny beckoned to him, Bumble came at once.

"Will you do something for me, Bumble?" whispered Johnny Chuck.

"Of course, I will," replied Bumble, in his gruff voice. "What is it?"

Then Johnny Chuck told Bumble the Bee how Granny and Reddy Fox were waiting for him to come out for his breakfast and how they had planned to gobble him up for their own breakfast. Bumble the Bee grew very indignant.

"What do you want me to do, Johnny Chuck?" he asked. "If I can help you, just tell me how."

Johnny whispered something to Bumble the Bee, and Bumble laughed right out loud. Then he buzzed up out of the doorway, and Johnny crept up to watch. Straight over to where Reddy Fox was squatting behind the clump of grass flew Bumble the Bee, so swiftly that Johnny could hardly see him. Suddenly Reddy gave a yelp and sprang into the air. Johnny Chuck clapped both hands over his mouth to keep from laughing out loud, for you see Bumble the Bee had stuck his sharp little lance into one of the ears of Reddy Fox.

Granny Fox looked up and scowled. "Keep still," she whispered.

Just then Reddy yelped louder than before, the Bumble had stung him in the other ear.

"What's the matter?" snapped Granny Fox.

"I don't know," cried Reddy Fox, hanging on to both ears.

"You are—" began Granny Fox, but Johnny Chuck never knew what she was going to say Reddy Fox was, for you see just then Bumble the Bee thrust his sharp little lance into one of her ears, and before she could turn around he had done the same thing to the other ear.

Granny Fox didn't wait for any more. She started off as fast as she could go, with Reddy Fox after her, and every few steps they rubbed their ears and shook their heads as if they thought they could shake out the pain.

X
Billy Mink Goes Dinnerless

DOWN the Laughing Brook came Billy Mink. He was feeling very good that morning, was Billy Mink, pleased with the world in general and with himself in particular. When he reached the Smiling Pool he swam out to the Big Rock. Little Joe Otter was already there, and not far away, lazily floating, with his head and back out of water, was Jerry Muskrat.

"Hello, Billy Mink," cried Little Joe Otter.

"Hello yourself," replied Billy Mink, with a grin.

"Where are you going?" asked Little Joe Otter.

"Nowhere in particular," replied Billy Mink.

"Let's go fishing down to the Big River," said Little Joe Otter.

"Let's!" cried Billy, diving from the highest point on the Big Rock.

So off they started across the Green Meadows towards the Big River. Half way there they met Reddy Fox.

"Hello, Reddy! Come on with us to the Big River, fishing," called Billy Mink.

Now Reddy Fox is no fisherman, though he likes fish to eat well enough. He remembered the last time he went fishing and how Billy Mink had laughed at him when he fell into the Smiling Pool. He was just about to say "no" when he changed his mind.

"All right, I'll go," said Reddy Fox.

So the three of them raced merrily across the Green Meadows until they came to the Big River. Now Billy Mink and Little Joe Otter are famous fishermen and can swim even faster than the fish themselves. But Reddy Fox is a poor swimmer and must depend upon his wits. When they reached the bank of the Big River they very carefully crawled down to a sandy beach. There, just a little way out from shore, a school of little striped perch were at play. Billy Mink and Little Joe Otter prepared to dive in and each grab a fish, but Reddy Fox knew that he could not swim well enough for that.

"Wait a minute," whispered Reddy. "Billy Mink, you go up the river a little way and swim out beyond where the fish are at play. Little Joe Otter, you go down the river a little way and swim out to join Billy Mink. Then both together rush in as fast as you can swim. The fish will be so frightened they will rush in where the water is shallow. Of course you will each catch one, anyway, and perhaps I may be so lucky as to catch one in the shallow water."

Billy Mink and Little Joe Otter agreed, and did just as Reddy Fox had told them to. When they were between the playing fish and deep water they

"Come on with us to the Big River, fishing,"
called Billy Mink. *See page 69.*

started in with a rush. The little striped perch were young and foolish. When they saw Billy Mink and Little Joe Otter they rushed madly away from them without looking to see where they were going to. As Reddy Fox had foreseen would be the case, a lot of them became stranded where the water was too shallow for swimming, and there they jumped and flapped helplessly.

Reddy was waiting for them and in a twinkling his little black paw had scooped half a dozen fish high and dry on the beach. Billy Mink and Little Joe Otter were too busy watching the fish to see what Reddy was doing. He had caught six fish and these he hid under a log. When Billy Mink and Little Joe Otter swam ashore, Reddy was the picture of disappointment, for he had nothing to show, while the others each had a plump little fish.

"Never mind," said Little Joe Otter, "I'll give you the next one I catch."

But Billy Mink jeered at Reddy Fox. "Pooh! you're no fisherman, Reddy Fox! If I couldn't catch fish when they are chased right into my hands I'd never go fishing."

Reddy Fox pretended to be indignant. "I tell you what, Billy Mink," said he, "if I don't catch more fish than you do to-day I'll bring you the plumpest chicken in Farmer Brown's dooryard, but if I do catch more fish than you do you will give me the biggest one you catch. Do you agree?"

Now Billy Mink is very fond of plump chicken

and here was a chance to get one without danger of meeting Bowser the Hound, who guards Farmer Brown's chickens. So Billy Mink agreed to give Reddy Fox the biggest fish he caught that day if Reddy could show more fish than he could at the end of the day. All the time he chuckled to himself, for you know Billy Mink is a famous fisherman, and he knew that Reddy Fox is a poor swimmer and does not like the water.

By and by they came to another sandy beach like the first one. They could see another school of foolish young fish at play. As before, Reddy Fox remained on shore while the others swam out and drove the fish in. As before Reddy caught half a dozen, while Billy Mink and Little Joe Otter each caught one this time. Reddy hid five and then pretended to be so tickled over catching one, the smallest of the lot, that Billy Mink didn't once suspect a trick.

Two or three times more Reddy Fox repeated this. Then he discovered a big pickerel sunning himself beside an old log floating in deep water. Reddy couldn't catch Mr. Pickerel, for the water was deep. What should he do? Reddy sat down to think. Finally he thought of a plan. Very cautiously he backed away so as not to scare the big fish. Then he called Billy Mink. When Billy saw the big pickerel, his mouth watered, too, and his little black eyes sparkled.

Very quietly Billy slipped into the water back of

the old log. There was not so much as a ripple to warn the big pickerel. Drawing a long breath, Billy dived under the log, and coming up under the big pickerel, seized it by the middle. There was a tremendous thrashing and splashing, and then Billy Mink swam ashore and proudly laid the big fish on the bank.

"Don't you wish it was yours?" asked Billy Mink.

"It ought to be mine, for I saw it first," said Reddy Fox.

"But you didn't catch it and I did," retorted Billy Mink. "I'm going to have it for my dinner. My, but I do like fat pickerel!" Billy smacked his lips.

Reddy Fox said nothing, but tried his best to look disappointed and dejected. All the time he was chuckling inwardly.

For the rest of the day the fishing was poor. Just as Old Mother West Wind started for the Green Meadows to take her children, the Merry Little Breezes, to their home behind the Purple Hills, the three little fishermen started to count up their catch. Then Reddy brought out all the fish that he had hidden. When they saw the pile of fish Reddy Fox had, Billy Mink and Little Joe Otter were so surprised that their eyes popped out and their jaws dropped. Very foolish they looked, very foolish indeed, for Reddy had four times as many as either of them.

Reddy walked over to the big pickerel and picking it up, carried it over to his pile. "What are you doing with my fish?" shouted Billy Mink angrily.

"It's isn't yours, it's mine!" retorted Reddy Fox.

Billy Mink fairly danced up and down he was so angry. "It's not yours!" he shrieked. "It's mine, for I caught it!"

"And you agreed that your biggest fish should be mine if I caught more fish than you did. I've caught four times as many, so the pickerel is mine," retorted Reddy, winking at Little Joe Otter.

Then Billy Mink did a very foolish thing; he lost his temper completely. He called Reddy Fox bad names. But he did not dare try to take the big pickerel away from Reddy, for Reddy is much bigger than he. Finally he worked himself into such a rage that he ran off home leaving his pile of fish behind.

Reddy Fox and Little Joe Otter took care not to touch Billy Mink's fish, but Reddy divided his big pile with Little Joe Otter. Then they, too, started for home, Reddy carrying the big pickerel.

Late that night, when he had recovered his temper, Billy Mink began to grow hungry. The more he thought of his fish the hungrier he grew. Finally he could stand it no longer and started for the Big River to see what had become of his fish. He reached the strip of beach where he had so foolishly left them just in time to see the last striped perch disappear down the long throat of Mr. Night Heron.

And this is how it happened that Billy Mink went

dinnerless to bed. But he had learned three things, had Billy, and he never forgot them—that wit is often better than skill; that it is not only mean but is very foolish to sneer at another; and that to lose one's temper is the most foolish thing in the world.

XI
Grandfather Frog's Journey

GRANDFATHER Frog sat on his big green lily-pad in the Smiling Pool and—Grandfather Frog was asleep! There was no doubt about it, Grandfather Frog was really and truly asleep. His hands were folded across his white and yellow waistcoat and his eyes were closed. Three times the Merry Little Breezes blew a foolish green fly right past his nose;—Grandfather Frog didn't so much as blink.

Presently Billy Mink discovered that Grandfather Frog was asleep. Billy's little black eyes twinkled with mischief as he hurried over to the slippery slide in search of Little Joe Otter. Then the two scamps hunted up Jerry Muskrat. They found him very busy storing away a supply of food in his new house. At first Jerry refused to listen to what they had to say, but the more they talked the more Jerry became interested.

"We won't hurt Grandfather Frog, not the least little big," protested Billy Mink. "It will be just the best joke and the greatest fun ever, and no harm done."

The more Jerry thought over Billy Mink's plan, the funnier the joke seemed. Finally Jerry agreed to join Billy Mink and Little Joe Otter. Then the three put their heads together and with a lot of giggling and chuckling they planned their joke on Grandfather Frog.

Now Jerry Muskrat can stay a very long time under water, and his teeth are long and sharp in order to cut the roots on which he depends for much of his food. So Jerry swam out to the big green lily-pad on which sat Grandfather Frog fast asleep. Diving way to the bottom of the Smiling Pool, Jerry cut off the stem of the big green lily-pad close to its root way down in the mud.

While Jerry was at work doing this, Billy Mink sent the Merry Little Breezes hurrying over the Green Meadows to call all the little meadow people to the Smiling Pool. Then, when Jerry Muskrat came up for a breath of air, Billy Mink dived down and, getting hold of the end of the lily-pad stem, he began to swim, towing the big green lily-pad after him very slowly and gently so as not to waken Grandfather Frog. When Billy had to come up for air, Little Joe Otter took his place. Then Jerry Muskrat took his turn.

Across the Smiling Pool, past the Big Rock, they towed the big green lily-pad, while Grandfather Frog slept peacefully, his hands folded over his white and yellow waistcoat. Past the bulrushes and Jerry Muskrat's new house, past Little Joe Otter's slippery slide sailed Grandfather Frog, and still he slept and dreamed of the days when the world was young.

Out of the Smiling Pool and into the Laughing Brook, where the brown water flows smoothly, the three little swimmers towed the big green lily-pad. It floated along of itself now, and all they had to do was to steer it clear of rocks and old logs. Once it almost got away from them, on the edge of a tiny waterfall, but all three pulling together towed it out of danger. At last, in a dear little pool with a mossy green bank, they anchored the big green lily-pad.

Then Billy Mink hurried back to the Smiling Pool to tell the little meadow people where to find Grandfather Frog. Little Joe Otter climbed out on the mossy green bank and Jerry Muskrat joined him there to rest and dry off. One by one the little meadow people came hurrying up. Reddy Fox was the first. Then came Johnny Chuck and Striped Chipmunk. Of course Peter Rabbit was on hand. You can always count Peter in, when there is anything going on among the little meadow people. Danny Meadow Mouse and Happy Jack Squirrel arrived quite out of breath. Sammy Jay and Blacky the Crow were not far behind, Last of all came Jimmy Skunk, who never hurries.

Each in turn peeped over the edge of the mossy green bank to see Grandfather Frog still sleeping peacefully on his big green lily-pad in the dear little pool. Then all hid where they could see him when he awoke, but where he could not see them.

Presently Billy Mink reached out with a long straw and tickled Grandfather Frog on the end of his nose. Grandfather Frog opened his eyes and yawned sleepily. Right over his head he saw jolly, round, red Mr. Sun smiling down on him just as he last saw him before falling asleep. He yawned again and then looked to see if Billy Mink was sitting on the Big Rock.

Where was the Big Rock? Grandfather Frog sat up very suddenly and rubbed his eyes. There wasn't any Big Rock! Grandfather Frog pinched himself to make sure that he was awake. Then he rubbed his eyes again and looked down at the big green lily-pad. Yes, that was his, the very same lily-pad on which he sat every day.

Grandfather Frog was more perplexed than ever. Slowly he looked around. Where were the slippery slide and Jerry Muskrat's new house? Where were the bulrushes and where—where was the *Smiling Pool?* Grandfather Frog's jaw dropped as he looked about him. His own big green lily-pad was the only lily-pad in sight. Had the world turned topsy-turvy while he slept?

"Chug-a-rum!" said Grandfather Frog. "This is very strange, very strange, indeed!"

Then he turned around three times and pinched himself again. "Very strange, very strange, indeed," muttered Grandfather Frog over and over again. He scratched his head first with one hand and then with the other, and the more he scratched the stranger it all seemed.

Just then he heard a giggle up on the mossy

green bank. Grandfather Frog whirled around. "Chug-a-rum!" he exclaimed. "Billy Mink, come out from behind that tall grass and tell me where I am and what this means! I might have known that you were at the bottom of it."

Then out jumped all the little meadow people and the Merry Little Breezes to shout and laugh and dance and roll over and over on the mossy green bank. Grandfather Frog looked at one and then at another and gradually he began to smile. Pretty soon he was laughing as hard as any of them, as Billy Mink told how they had towed him down to the dear little pool.

"And now, Grandfather Frog, we'll take you home again," concluded Billy Mink.

So, as before, Billy Mink and Little Joe Otter and Jerry Muskrat took turns towing the big green lily-pad, while in the middle of it sat Grandfather Frog, catching foolish green flies which the Merry Little Breezes blew over to him.

Reddy Fox, Johnny Chuck, Peter Rabbit, Danny Meadow Mouse, Striped Chipmunk, Happy Jack Squirrel and Jimmy Skunk raced and capered along the bank and shouted encouragement to the three little swimmers, while overhead flew Sammy Jay and Blacky the Crow. And, never once losing his balance, Grandfather Frog sat on the big green lily-pad, enjoying his strange ride and smacking his lips over the foolish green flies.

And so they came once more to the Smiling Pool,

past the slippery slide, past the bulrushes and Jerry Muskrat's new house and the Big Rock, until Grandfather Frog and his queer craft were once more anchored safe and sound in the old familiar place.

"Chug-a-rum!" said Grandfather Frog. "I think I'd like to go again."

XII
Why Blacky the Crow Wears Mourning

GRANDFATHER Frog sat on his big green lily-pad in the Smiling Pool. Grandfather Frog felt very good that morning, very good indeed, because—why, because his white and yellow waistcoat was full of foolish green flies. It is doubtful, very, very doubtful if Grandfather Frog could have swallowed another foolish green fly to save his life. So he sat with his hands folded across his white and yellow waistcoat, and into his eyes, his great goggly eyes, there crept a far, far, far away look. Grandfather Frog was dreaming of the days when the world was young and the frogs ruled the world.

Pretty soon the Merry Little Breezes of Old Mother West Wind came over to the Smiling Pool to rock Mrs. Redwing's babies to sleep in their cradle in the bulrushes. But when they saw Grandfather Frog they forgot all about Mrs. Redwing and her babies.

"Good morning, Grandfather Frog!" they shouted.

Grandfather Frog awoke from his dream with a funny little jump.

"Goodness, how you startled me!" said Grandfather Frog, smoothing down his white and yellow waistcoat.

The Merry Little Breezes giggled. "We didn't mean to, truly we didn't," said the merriest one of all. "We just wanted to know how you do this fine morning, and—and—"

"Chug-a-rum," said Grandfather Frog, "you want me to tell you a story."

The Merry Little Breezes giggled again. "How did you ever guess it?" they cried. "It must be because you are so very, very wise. Will you tell us a story, Grandfather Frog? Will you please?"

Grandfather Frog looked up and winked one big, goggly eye at jolly, round, red Mr. Sun, who was smiling down from the blue sky. Then he sat still so long that the Merry Little Breezes began to fear that Grandfather Frog was out of sorts and that there would be no story that morning. They fidgeted about among the bulrushes and danced back and forth across the lily-pads. They had even begun to think again of Mrs. Redwing's babies.

"Chug-a-rum!" said Grandfather Frog suddenly. "What shall I tell you about?"

Just then a black shadow swept across the Smiling Pool. "Caw, caw, caw, caw!" shouted Blacky the Crow noisily, as he flew over toward Farmer Brown's cornfield.

"Tell us why Blacky the Crow always wears a coat of black, as if he were in mourning," shouted the Merry Little Breezes.

Grandfather Frog watched Blacky disappear behind the Lone Pine. Then, when the Merry Little

Breezes had settled down, each in the golden heart of a white water-lily, he began:

"Once upon a time, when the world was young, old Mr. Crow, the grandfather a thousand times removed of Blacky, whom you all know, lived in the Green Forest on the edge of the Green Meadows, just as Blacky does now, and with him lived his brothers and sisters, his uncles and aunts, his cousins and all his poor relations.

"Now Mr. Crow was very smart. Indeed, he was the smartest of all the birds. There wasn't anything that old Mr. Crow couldn't do or didn't know. At least he thought there wasn't. All the little meadow people and forest folks began to think so, too, and one after another they got in the habit of coming to him for advice, until pretty soon they were bringing all their affairs to Mr. Crow for settlement.

"Now for a while Mr. Crow showed great wisdom, and this so pleased Old Mother Nature that she gave him a suit of pure, dazzling white, so that all seeing him might look up to him as a shining example of wisdom and virtue. Of course all his brothers and sisters, his uncles and aunts, his cousins and all his poor relations at once put on white, that all might know that they were of Mr. Crow's family. And of course every one showed them the greatest attention out of respect to old Mr. Crow, so that presently they began to hold their heads very high and to think that because they were related to old Mr. Crow they were a little better than any of the other little meadow people and forest folks. When they met old Mr. Rabbit they would pretend not to see him, because he wore a white patch on the seat of his trousers. When old Mr. Woodchuck said 'good morning,' they would pretend not to hear, for you know Mr. Woodchuck wore a suit of dingy yellow and lived in a hole in the ground. Old Mr. Toad was ugly to look upon. Besides, he worked for his living in a garden. So when they happened to meet him on the road they always turned their backs.

"For a long time old Mr. Crow himself continued to be a very fine gentleman and to hold the respect of all his neighbors. He was polite to every one, and to all who came to him he freely gave of his advice as wisely as he knew how. Of course it wasn't long before he knew all about his neighbors and their private affairs. Now it isn't safe to know too much about your neighbors and what they are doing. It is dangerous knowledge, very dangerous knowledge indeed," said Grandfather Frog solemnly.

"To be sure it would have been safe enough," he continued, "if Mr. Crow had kept it to himself. But after a while Mr. Crow became vain. Yes, Sir, that is just what happened to old Mr. Crow—he became vain. He liked to feel that all the little meadow people and forest folks looked up to him with respect, and whenever he saw one of them coming he would brush his white coat, swell himself up and look very important. After a while he began to brag among his relatives of how much he knew about his neighbors. Of course they were very much interested, very much interested indeed, and this flattered Mr. Crow so that almost before he knew it he was telling some of the private affairs which had been brought to him for his advice. Oh, dear me, Mr. Crow began to gossip.

"Now, gossiping is one of the worst habits in all the world, one of the very worst. No good ever comes of it. It just makes trouble, trouble, trouble. It was so now. Mr. Crow's relatives repeated the stories that they heard. But they took great care that no one should know where they came from. My, my, my, how trouble did spread on the Green Meadows and in the Green Forest! No one suspected old Mr. Crow, so he was more in demand than ever to straighten matters out. His neighbors came to him so much that they began to be ashamed to ask his advice for nothing, so they brought him presents so that no more need Mr. Crow hunt for things to eat. Instead, he lived on the fat of the land without working, and grew fat and lazy.

"As I have told you, Mr. Crow was smart. Yes, indeed, he certainly was smart. It did not take him long to see that the more trouble there was among his neighbors the more they would need his advice, and the more they needed his advice the more presents he would receive. He grew very crafty. He would tell tales just to make trouble, and sometimes, when he saw a chance, he would give advice that he knew would make more trouble. The fact is, old Mr. Crow became a mischief-maker, the very worst kind of a mischief-maker. And all the time he appeared to be the fine gentleman that he used to be. He wore his fine white coat as proudly as ever.

"Matters grew worse and worse. Never had there been so much trouble on the Green Meadows or so many quarrels in the Green Forest. Old Mr. Mink never met old Mr. Otter without picking a fight. Old Mrs. Skunk wouldn't speak to old Mrs. Coon. Old Mr. Chipmunk turned his back on his cousin, old Mr. Red Squirrel, whenever their paths crossed. Even my grandfather a thousand times removed, old Mr. Frog, refused to see his nearest relative, old Mr. Toad. And all the time old Mr. Crow wore his beautiful suit of white and grew rich and fat, chuckling to himself over his ill-gotten wealth.

"Then one day came Old Mother Nature to visit the Green Meadows. It didn't take her long to find that something was wrong, very wrong indeed. Old Mr. Crow and all his relatives hastened to pay their respects and to tell her how much they appreciated their beautiful white suits. Old Mr. Crow made a full report of all the troubles that had been brought to him, but he took great care not to let her know that he had had any part in making trouble. He looked very innocent, oh, very, very innocent, but not once did he look her straight in the face.

"Now the eyes of Old Mother Nature are wonderfully sharp and they seemed to bore right through old Mr. Crow. You can't fool Old Mother Nature. No, Sir, you can't fool Old Mother Nature, and it's of no use to try. She listened to all that Mr. Crow had to say. Then she sent Mr. North Wind to blow his great trumpet and call together all the little people of the Green Meadows and all the little folks of the Green Forest.

"When they had all come together she told them all that had happened. She told just how Mr. Crow had started the stories in order to make trouble so that they would seek his advice and bring him presents to pay for it. When the neighbors of old Mr. Crow heard this they were very angry, and they demanded of Old Mother Nature that Mr. Crow be punished.

"'Look!' said Old Mother Nature, pointing at old Mr. Crow. 'He has been punished already.'

"Every one turned to look at Mr. Crow. At first they hardly knew him. Instead of his suit of spotless white his clothes were black, as black as the blackest night. So were the clothes of his uncles and aunts, his brothers and sisters, his cousins and all his poor relations.

"And ever since that long-ago day, when the world was young, the Crows have been mischief-makers and have worn black, that all who look may know that they bring nothing but trouble," concluded Grandfather Frog.

"Thank you! Thank you, Grandfather Frog," shouted the Merry Little Breezes, jumping up to go rock the Redwing babies.

"Caw, caw, caw, caw!" shouted Blacky the Crow, flying over their heads with a mouthful of corn he had stolen from Farmer Brown's cornfield.

XIII
Striped Chipmunk Fools Peter Rabbit

PETER Rabbit sat at the top of the Crooked Little Path where it starts down the hill. He was sitting there when jolly, round, red Mr. Sun threw his nightcap off and began his daily climb up into the blue, blue sky. He saw Old Mother West Wind hurry down from the Purple Hills and turn her Merry Little Breezes out to play on the Green Meadows.

Peter yawned. The fact is, Peter had been out nearly all night, and now he didn't know just what to do with himself. Presently he saw Striped Chipmunk whisk up on top of an old log. As usual the pockets in Striped Chipmunk's cheeks were stuffed so full that his head looked to be twice as big as it really is, and as usual he seemed to be very busy, very busy indeed. He stopped just long enough to wink one of his saucy black eyes and shout: "Good morning, Peter Rabbit!"

Then he disappeared as suddenly as he had come. A few minutes later he was back on the old log, but this time his cheeks were empty.

"Fine day, Peter Rabbit," said Striped Chipmunk, and whisked out of sight.

Peter Rabbit yawned again. Then he closed his

eyes for just a minute. When he opened them there was Striped Chipmunk on the old log just as before, and the pockets in both cheeks were so full that it seemed as if they would burst.

"Nice morning to work, Peter Rabbit," said Striped Chipmunk, in spite of his full cheeks. Then he was gone.

Once more Peter Rabbit closed his eyes, but hardly were they shut when Striped Chipmunk shouted:

"Oh, you Peter Rabbit, been out all night?"

Peter snapped his eyes open just in time to see the funny little tail of Striped Chipmunk vanish over the side of the old log. Peter scratched one of his long ears and yawned again, for Peter was growing more and more sleepy. It was a long yawn, but Peter cut it off right in the middle, for there was Striped Chipmunk back on the old log, and both pockets in his cheeks were stuffed full.

Now Peter Rabbit is as curious as he is lazy, and you know he is very, very lazy. The fact is, Peter Rabbit's curiosity is his greatest fault, and it gets him into a great deal of trouble. It is because of this and the bad, bad habit of meddling in the affairs of other people into which it has led him that Peter Rabbit has such long ears.

For a while Peter watched busy Striped Chipmunk. Then he began to wonder what Striped Chipmunk could be doing. The more he wondered the more he felt that he really must know. The next time Striped Chipmunk appeared on the old log, Peter shouted to him.

"Hi, Striped Chipmunk, what are you so busy about? Why don't you play a little?"

Striped Chipmunk stopped a minute. "I'm building a new house," said he.

"Where?" asked Peter Rabbit.

"That's telling," replied Striped Chipmunk, and whisked out of sight.

Now Peter Rabbit knew where Reddy Fox and Jimmy Skunk and Bobby Coon and Happy Jack Squirrel and Johnny Chuck and Danny Meadow Mouse lived. He knew all the little paths leading to their homes. But he did not know where Striped Chipmunk lived. He never had known. He thought of this as he watched Striped Chipmunk hurrying back and forth. The more he thought of it the more curious he grew. He really *must* know. Pretty soon along came Jimmy Skunk, looking for some beetles.

"Hello, Jimmy Skunk," said Peter Rabbit.

"Hello, Peter Rabbit," said Jimmy Skunk.

"Do you know where Striped Chipmunk lives?" asked Peter Rabbit.

"No, I don't know where Striped Chipmunk lives, and I don't care; it's none of my business," replied Jimmy Skunk. "Have you seen any beetles this morning?"

Peter Rabbit hadn't seen any beetles, so Jimmy Skunk went on down the Crooked Little Path, still looking for his breakfast.

By and by along came Johnny Chuck.

"Hello, Johnny Chuck!" said Peter Rabbit.

"Hello, yourself!" said Johnny Chuck.

"Do you know where Striped Chipmunk lives?" asked Peter Rabbit.

"No, I don't, for it's none of my business," said Johnny Chuck, and started on down the Crooked Little Path to the Green Meadows.

Then along came Bobby Coon.

"Hello, Bobby Coon!" said Peter Rabbit.

"Hello!" replied Bobby Coon shortly, for he too had been out all night and was very sleepy.

"Do you know where Striped Chipmunk lives?" asked Peter Rabbit.

"Don't know and don't want to; it's none of my business," said Bobby Coon even more shortly than before, and started on for his hollow chestnut tree to sleep the long, bright day away.

Peter Rabbit could stand it no longer. Curiosity had driven away all desire to sleep. He simply had to know where Striped Chipmunk lived.

"I'll just follow Striped Chipmunk and see for myself where he lives," said Peter to himself.

So Peter Rabbit hid behind a tuft of grass close by the old log and sat very, very still. It was a very good place to hide, a very good place. Probably if Peter Rabbit had not been so brimming over with curiosity he would have succeeded in escaping the sharp eyes of Striped Chipmunk. But people full of curiosity are forever pricking up their ears to hear things which do not in the least concern them. It was so with Peter Rabbit. He was so afraid that he would miss something that both his long ears were standing up straight, and they came above the grass behind which Peter Rabbit was hiding.

Of course Striped Chipmunk saw them the very instant he jumped up on the old log with both pockets in his cheeks stuffed full. He didn't say a word, but his sharp little eyes twinkled as he jumped off the end of the old log and scurried along under the bushes, for he guessed what Peter Rabbit was hiding for, and though he did not once turn his head he knew that Peter was following him. You see Peter runs with his jumps, lipperty-lipperty-lip, and people who jump must make a noise.

So, though he tried very hard not to make a sound, Peter was in such a hurry to keep Striped Chipmunk in sight that he really made a great deal of noise. The more noise Peter made, the more Striped Chipmunk chuckled to himself.

Presently Striped Chipmunk stopped. Then he sat up very straight and looked this way and looked that way, just as if trying to make sure that no one was watching him. Then he emptied two pocketfuls of shining yellow gravel on to a nice new mound which he was building. Once more he sat up and looked this way and looked that way. Then he scuttled back towards the old log. As he ran Striped Chipmunk chuckled and chuckled to himself, for all the time he had seen Peter Rabbit lying flat down behind a little bush and knew that Peter Rabbit was thinking to himself how smart he had been to find Striped Chipmunk's home when no one else knew where it was.

No sooner was Striped Chipmunk out of sight than up jumped Peter Rabbit. He smiled to himself as he hurried over to the shining mound of yellow gravel. You see Peter's curiosity was so great that not once did he think how mean he was to spy on Striped Chipmunk.

"Now," thought Peter, "I know where Striped Chipmunk lives. Jimmy Skunk doesn't know. Johnny Chuck doesn't know. Bobby Coon doesn't know. But *I* know. Striped Chipmunk may fool all the others, but he can't fool me."

By this time Peter Rabbit had reached the shining mound of yellow gravel. At once he began to hunt for the doorway to Striped Chipmunk's home. But there wasn't any doorway. No, Sir, there wasn't any doorway! Look as he would, Peter Rabbit could not find the least sign of a doorway. He walked 'round and 'round the mound and looked here and looked there, but not the least sign of a door was to be seen. There was nothing but the shining mound of yellow gravel, the green grass, the green bushes and the blue, blue sky, with jolly, round, red Mr. Sun looking down and laughing at him.

Peter Rabbit sat down on Striped Chipmunk's

Peter was so surprised that he nearly fell backward. *See page 98.*

shining mound of yellow gravel and scratched his left ear with his left hindfoot. Then he scratched his right ear with his right hindfoot. It was very perplexing. Indeed, it was so perplexing that Peter quite forgot that Striped Chipmunk would soon be coming back. Suddenly right behind Peter's back Striped Chipmunk spoke.

"How do you like my sand pile, Peter Rabbit? Don't you think it is a pretty nice sand pile?" asked Striped Chipmunk politely. And all the time he was chuckling away to himself.

Peter was so surprised that he very nearly fell backward off the shining mound of yellow gravel. For a minute he didn't know what to say. Then he found his tongue.

"Oh," said Peter Rabbit, apparently in the greatest surprise, "is this your sand pile, Striped Chipmunk? It's a very nice sand pile indeed. Is this where you live?"

Striped Chipmunk shook his head. "No, oh, my, no!" said he. "I wouldn't think of living in such an exposed place! My goodness, no indeed! Everybody knows where this is. I'm building a new home, you know, and of course I don't want the gravel to clutter up my dooryard. So I've brought it all here. Makes a nice sand pile, doesn't it? You are very welcome to sit on my sand pile whenever you feel like it, Peter Rabbit. It's a good place to take a sun bath; I hope you'll come often."

All the time Striped Chipmunk was saying this

his sharp little eyes twinkled with mischief and he chuckled softly to himself.

Peter Rabbit was more curious than ever. "Where is your new home, Striped Chipmunk?" he asked.

"Not far from here; come call on me," said Striped Chipmunk.

Then with a jerk of his funny little tail he was gone. It seemed as if the earth must have swallowed him up. Striped Chipmunk can move very quickly, and he had whisked out of sight in the bushes before Peter Rabbit could turn his head to watch him.

Peter looked behind every bush and under every stone, but nowhere could he find Striped Chipmunk or a sign of Striped Chipmunk's home, excepting the shining mound of yellow gravel. At last Peter pushed his inquisitive nose right into the doorway of Bumble the Bee. Now Bumble the Bee happened to be at home, and being very short of temper, he thrust a sharp little needle into the inquisitive nose of Peter Rabbit.

"Oh! oh! oh!" shrieked Peter, clapping both hands to his nose, and started off home as fast as he could go.

And though he didn't know it and doesn't know it to this day, he went right across the doorstep of Striped Chipmunk's home. So Peter still wonders and wonders where Striped Chipmunk lives, and no one can tell him, not even the Merry Little

Breezes. You see there is not even a sign of a path leading to his doorway, for Striped Chipmunk never goes or comes twice the same way. His doorway is very small, just large enough for him to squeeze through, and it is so hidden in the grass that often the Merry Little Breezes skip right over it without seeing it.

Every grain of sand and gravel from the fine long halls and snug chambers Striped Chipmunk has built underground he has carefully carried in the pockets in his cheeks to the shining mound of yellow gravel found by Peter Rabbit. Not so much as a grain is dropped on his doorstep to let his secret out.

So in and out among the little meadow people skips Striped Chipmunk all the long day, and not one has found out where he lives. But no one really cares excepting Peter Rabbit, who is still curious.

XIV
Jerry Muskrat's New House

JERRY Muskrat wouldn't play. Billy Mink had tried to get him to. Little Joe Otter had tried to get him to. The Merry Little Breezes had tried to get him to. It was of no use, no use at all. Jerry Muskrat wouldn't play.

"Come on, Jerry, come on play with us," they begged all together.

But Jerry shook his head. "Can't," said he.

"Why not? Won't your mother let you?" demanded Billy Mink, making a long dive into the Smiling Pool. He was up again in time to hear Jerry reply:

"Yes, my mother will let me. It isn't that. It's because we are going to have a long winter and a cold winter and I must prepare for it."

Every one laughed, every one except Great-Grandfather Frog, who sat on his big green lily-pad watching for foolish green flies.

"Pooh!" exclaimed Little Joe Otter. "A lot you know about it, Jerry Muskrat! Ho, ho, ho! A lot you know about it! Are you clerk of the weather? It is only fall now—what can you know about what the winter will be? Oh come, Jerry Muskrat, don't pretend to be so wise. I can swim twice across the

Smiling Pool while you are swimming across once—come on!"

Jerry Muskrat shook his head. "Haven't time," said he. "I tell you we are going to have a long winter and a hard winter, and I've got to prepare for it. When it comes you'll remember what I have told you."

Little Joe Otter made a wry face and slid down his slippery slide, splash into the Smiling Pool, throwing water all over Jerry Muskrat, who was sitting on the end of a log close by. Jerry shook the water from his coat, which is waterproof, you know. Everybody laughed, that is, everybody but Grandfather Frog. He did not even smile.

"Chug-a-rum!" said Grandfather Frog, who is very wise. "Jerry Muskrat knows. If Jerry says that we are going to have a long cold winter you may be sure that he knows what he is talking about."

Billy Mink turned a back somersault into the Smiling Pool so close to the big green lily-pad on which Grandfather Frog sat that the waves almost threw Grandfather Frog into the water.

"Pooh," said Billy Mink, "how can Jerry Muskrat know anything more about it than we do?"

Grandfather Frog looked at Billy Mink severely. He does not like Billy Mink, who has been known to gobble up some of Grandfather Frog's children when he thought that no one was looking.

"Old Mother Nature was here and told him," said Grandfather Frog gruffly.

"Oh!" exclaimed Billy Mink and Little Joe Otter together. "That's different," and they looked at Jerry Muskrat with greater respect.

"How are you going to prepare for the long cold winter, Jerry Muskrat?" asked one of the Merry Little Breezes.

"I'm going to build a house, a big, warm house," replied Jerry Muskrat, "and I'm going to begin right now."

Splash! Jerry had disappeared into the Smiling Pool. Presently, over on the far side where the water was shallow, it began to bubble and boil as if a great fuss was going on underneath the surface. Jerry Muskrat had begun work. The water grew muddy, very muddy indeed, so muddy that Little Joe Otter and Billy Mink climbed out on the Big Rock in disgust. When finally Jerry Muskrat swam out to rest on the end of a log they shouted to him angrily.

"Hi, Jerry Muskrat, you're spoiling our swimming water! What are you doing anyway?"

"I'm digging for the foundations for my new house, and it isn't your water any more than it's mine," replied Jerry Muskrat, drawing a long breath before he disappeared under water again.

The water grew muddier and muddier, until even Grandfather Frog began to look annoyed. Billy Mink and Little Joe Otter started off up the Laughing Brook, where the water was clear. The Merry Little Breezes danced away across the Green

"I'm going to build a house," replied Jerry Muskrat. *See page 103.*

Meadows to play with Johnny Chuck, and Grandfather Frog settled himself comfortably on his big green lily-pad to dream of the days when the world was young and the frogs ruled the world.

But Jerry Muskrat worked steadily, digging and piling sods in a circle for the foundation of his house. In the center he dug out a chamber from which he planned a long tunnel to his secret burrow far away in the bank, and another to the deepest part of the Smiling Pool, where even in the coldest weather the water would not freeze to the bottom as it would do in the shallow places.

All day long while Billy Mink and Little Joe Otter and the Merry Little Breezes and Johnny Chuck and Peter Rabbit and Danny Meadow Mouse and all the other little meadow people were playing or lazily taking sun naps, Jerry Muskrat worked steadily. Jolly, round, red Mr. Sun, looking down from the blue, blue sky, smiled to see how industrious the little fellow was. That evening, when Old Mother West Wind hurried across the Green Meadows on her way to her home behind the Purple Hills, she found Jerry Muskrat sitting on the end of a log eating his supper of fresh-water clams. Showing just above the water on the edge of the Smiling Pool was the foundation of Jerry Muskrat's new house.

The next morning Jerry was up and at work even before Old Mother West Wind, who is a very early riser, came down from the Purple Hills. Of course every one was interested to see how the new house was coming along and to offer advice.

"Are you going to build it all of mud?" asked one of the Merry Little Breezes.

"No," said Jerry Muskrat, "I'm going to use green alder twigs and willow shoots and bulrush stalks. It's going to be two stories high, with a room down deep under water and another room up above with a beautiful bed of grass and soft moss."

"That will be splendid!" cried the Merry Little Breezes.

Then one of them had an idea. He whispered to the other Little Breezes. They all giggled and clapped their hands. Then they hurried off to find Billy Mink and Little Joe Otter. They even hunted up Johnny Chuck and Peter Rabbit and Danny Meadow Mouse.

Jerry Muskrat was so busy that he paid no attention to any one or anything else. He was attending strictly to the business of building a house that would keep him warm and comfortable when the long cold winter should freeze up tight the Smiling Pool.

Pretty soon he was ready for some green twigs to use in the walls of the new house. He swam across the Smiling Pool to the Laughing Brook, where the alders grow, to cut the green twigs which he needed. What do you think he found when he got there? Why, the nicest little pile of green twigs, all cut ready to use, and Johnny Chuck cutting more.

"Hello, Jerry Muskrat," said Johnny Chuck. "I've cut all these green twigs for your new house. I hope you can use them."

Jerry was so surprised that he hardly knew what to say. He thanked Johnny Chuck, and with the bundle of green twigs swam back to his new house. When he had used the last one he swam across to the bulrushes on the edge of the Smiling Pool.

"Good morning, Jerry Muskrat," said some one almost hidden by a big pile of bulrushes, all nicely cut. "I want to help build the new house."

It was Danny Meadow Mouse.

Jerry Muskrat was more surprised than ever. "Oh, thank you, Danny Meadow Mouse, thank you!" he said, and pushing the pile of bulrushes before him he swam back to his new house.

When he had used the rushes, Jerry wanted some young willow shoots, so he started for the place where the willows grow. Before he reached them he heard some one shouting:

"Hi, Jerry Muskrat! See the pile of willow shoots I've cut for your new house." It was Peter Rabbit, who is never known to work.

Jerry Muskrat was more surprised than ever and so pleased that all he could say was, "Thank you, thank you, Peter Rabbit!"

Back to the new house he swam with the pile of young willow shoots. When he had placed them to suit him he sat up on the walls of his house to rest. He looked across the Smiling Pool. Then he rubbed his eyes and looked again. Could it be—yes, it certainly was a bundle of green alder twigs floating straight across the Smiling Pool towards the new house! When they got close to him Jerry spied a sharp little black nose pushing them along, and back of the little black nose twinkled two little black eyes.

"What are you doing with those alder twigs, Billy Mink?" cried Jerry.

"Bringing them for your new house," shouted Billy Mink, popping out from behind the bundle of alder twigs.

And that was the beginning of the busiest day that the Smiling Pool had ever known. Billy Mink brought more alder twigs and willow shoots and bulrushes as fast as Johnny Chuck and Peter Rabbit and Danny Meadow Mouse could cut them. Little Joe Otter brought sods and mud to hold them in place.

Thick and high grew the walls of the new house. In the upper part Jerry built the nicest little room, and lined it with grass and soft moss, so that he could sleep warm and comfortable through the long cold winter. Over all he built a strong, thick roof beautifully rounded.

An hour before it was time for Old Mother West Wind to come for the Merry Little Breezes, Jerry Muskrat's new house was finished. Then such a frolic as there was in and around the Smiling Pool! Little Joe Otter made a new slippery slide down one side of the roof. Billy Mink said that the new house was better to dive off of than the Big Rock. Then the two of them, with Jerry Muskrat, cut up all sorts of monkey-shines in the water, while Johnny Chuck, Peter Rabbit, Danny Meadow Mouse and the Merry Little Breezes danced on the shore and shouted themselves hoarse.

When at last jolly, round, red Mr. Sun went to bed behind the Purple Hills, and the black shadows crept ever so softly out across the Smiling Pool, Jerry Muskrat sat on the roof of his house eating his supper of fresh-water clams. He was very tired, was Jerry Muskrat, very tired indeed, but he was very happy, for now he had no fear of the long cold winter. Best of all his heart was full of love—love for his little playmates of the Smiling Pool and the Green Meadows.

XV
Peter Rabbit's Big Cousin

JUMPER the Hare had come down out of the Green Woods to the Green Meadows. He is first cousin to Peter Rabbit, you know, and he looks just like Peter, only he is twice as big. His legs are twice as long and he can jump twice as far.

All the little meadow people were very polite to Jumper the Hare, all but Reddy Fox, who is never polite to any one unless he has a favor to ask. Peter Rabbit was very proud of his big cousin, very proud indeed. He showed Jumper the Hare all the secret paths in the Green Forest and across the Green Meadows. He took him to the Smiling Pool and the Laughing Brook, and everywhere Jumper the Hare was met with the greatest politeness.

But Jumper the Hare was timid, oh, very timid indeed. Every few jumps he sat up very straight to look this way and look that way, and to listen with his long ears. He jumped nervously at the least little noise. Yes, Sir, Jumper the Hare certainly was very timid.

"He's a coward!" sneered Reddy Fox.

And Billy Mink and Little Joe Otter and Jimmy Skunk, even Johnny Chuck, seeing Jumper the Hare duck and dodge at the shadow of Blacky the

Crow, agreed with Reddy Fox. Still, they were polite to him for the sake of Peter Rabbit and because Jumper really was such a big, handsome fellow. But behind his back they laughed at him. Even little Danny Meadow Mouse laughed.

Now it happened that Jumper the Hare had lived all his life in the Great Woods, where Mr. Panther and Tufty the Lynx and fierce Mr. Fisher were always hunting him, but where the shadows were deep and where there were plenty of places to hide. Indeed, his whole life had been a game of hide and seek, and always he had been the one sought. So on the Green Meadows, where hiding places were few and far between, Jumper the Hare was nervous.

But the little meadow people, not knowing this, thought him a coward, and while they were polite to him they had little to do with him, for no one really likes a coward. Peter Rabbit, however, could see no fault in his big cousin. He showed him where Farmer Brown's tender young carrots grow, and the shortest way to the cabbage patch. He made him acquainted with all his own secret hiding places in the old brier patch.

Then one bright sunny morning something happened. Johnny Chuck saw it. Jimmy Skunk saw it. Happy Jack Squirrel saw it. Sammy Jay saw it. And they told all the others.

Very early that morning Reddy Fox had started out to hunt for his breakfast. He was tiptoeing softly along the edge of the Green Forest looking for wood mice when whom should he see but Peter Rabbit. Peter was getting his breakfast in the sweet-clover bed, just beyond the old brier patch.

Reddy Fox squatted down behind a bush to watch. Peter Rabbit looked plump and fat. Reddy Fox licked his chops. "Peter Rabbit would make a better breakfast than wood mice, a very much better breakfast," said Reddy Fox to himself. Besides, he owed Peter Rabbit a grudge. He had not forgotten how Peter had tried to save his little brother from Reddy by bringing up Bowser the Hound.

Reddy Fox licked his chops again. He looked this way and he looked that way, but he could see no one watching. Old Mother West Wind had gone about her business. The Merry Little Breezes were over at the Smiling Pool to pay their respects to Great-Grandfather Frog. Even jolly, round, red Mr. Sun was behind a cloud. From his hiding place Reddy could not see Johnny Chuck or Jimmy Skunk or Happy Jack Squirrel or Sammy Jay. "No one will know what becomes of Peter Rabbit," thought Reddy Fox.

Very cautiously Reddy Fox crept out from behind the bush into the tall meadow grass. Flat on his stomach he crawled inch by inch. Every few minutes he stopped to listen and to peep over at the sweet-clover bed. There sat Peter Rabbit, eating, eating, eating the tender young clover as if he hadn't a care in the world but to fill his little round stomach.

Nearer and nearer crawled Reddy Fox. Now he was almost near enough to spring. "Thump, thump, thump!" The sound came from the brier patch.

"Thump, thump!"

This was Peter Rabbit hitting the ground with one of his hind feet. He had stopped eating and was sitting up very straight.

"Thump, thump, thump!" came the signal from the brier patch.

"Thump, thump!" responded Peter Rabbit, and started to run.

With a snarl Reddy Fox sprang after him. Then the thing happened. Reddy Fox caught a glimpse of something going over him and at the same time he received a blow that rolled him over and over in the grass.

In an instant he was on his feet and had whirled about, his eyes yellow with anger. There right in front of him sat Jumper the Hare. Reddy Fox could hardly believe his own eyes! Could it be that Jumper the Hare, the coward, had dared to strike him such a blow? Reddy forgot all about Peter Rabbit. With a snarl he rushed at Jumper the Hare.

Then it happened again. As light as a feather Jumper leaped over him, and as he passed, those big hind legs, at which Reddy Fox had laughed, came back with a kick that knocked all the breath out of Reddy Fox.

Reddy Fox was furious. Twice more he sprang, and twice more he was sent sprawling, with the breath knocked out of his body. That was enough. Tucking his tail between his legs, Reddy Fox sneaked away towards the Green Forest. As he ran he heard Peter Rabbit thumping in the old brier patch.

"I'm safe," signaled Peter Rabbit.

"Thump, thump, thump, thump! The coast is clear," replied Jumper the Hare.

Reddy Fox looked back from the edge of the Green Forest and gnashed his teeth. Peter Rabbit and Jumper the Hare were rubbing noses and contentedly eating tender young clover leaves.

"Now who's the coward?" jeered Sammy Jay from the top of the Lone Pine.

Reddy Fox said nothing, but slunk out of sight. Late that afternoon he sat on the hill at the top of the Crooked Little Path, and looked down on the Green Meadows. Over near the Smiling Pool were gathered all the little meadow people having the jolliest time in the world. While he watched they joined hands in a big circle and began to dance, Johnny Chuck, Jimmy Skunk, Bobby Coon, Little Joe Otter, Billy Mink, Happy Jack Squirrel, Striped Chipmunk, Danny Meadow Mouse, Peter Rabbit, Spotty the Turtle, even Great-Grandfather Frog and old Mr. Toad. And in the middle, sitting very straight, was Jumper the Hare.

And since that day Peter Rabbit has been prouder than ever of his big cousin, Jumper the Hare, for now no one calls him a coward.

THE END